THE SUNDAY SCHOOL TEACHER

COLE HART

COLE HART SIGNATURE

DEDICATION

Therefore, I tell you, whatever you ask for in prayer, believe that you have received it, and it will be yours. Mark 11:24

1

*I*t's rare, but sometimes it does get really cold in Atlanta. So cold that your teeth would chatter like a woodpecker tapping on a tree on a warm spring afternoon. That morning definitely wasn't a spring morning; instead, it was a chilling winter morning. The wind was whistling and whipping through the air, singing a tune like an old man downtown on the corner trying to raise money for his next meal. On that early bright Sunday morning, it was too cold for anyone; especially, Daisy Mae, an elderly woman, to be walking down Hosea Williams Drive in Kirkwood. She was in her late seventies, and even with wrinkles, crow feet at the corner of each of her eyes, saggy skin around her face and neck, she still looked good for her age. She had slight breathing problems, but that didn't detour her from trenching down Hosea Williams Drive like she was a young woman in great health.

Dressed in a navy-blue dress, underneath a waist length wool pea coat that gave off a lingering moth ball scent, mixed with an aroma of Ben Gay rubbing cream, Daisy Mae walked with a slight limp. It was more of a side to side wobble like a Penguin, with her leather back Bible carefully cuffed in her left arm as if she was going to school. Traffic was moving past her at a steady pace. She turned her head, looking toward moving cars that passed her and even waved her hand, her eyes were weak, not strong looking like they were ten, twenty, thirty years ago.

Daisy Mae, paused in her tracks for a brief moment, she touched her big hat on top of her head to make sure that it was still fitting right. Then, she took a couple of deep breaths just like her doctor had told her to, so she could catch her breath. He'd warned her about walking outside in the cold winter weather, but the old lady was stubborn and hard headed. Once she was at a complete stop, her chest was rising and falling as she breathed in deeply. She looked up the street, at the church in a distance, but there were spots flashing before her eyes. She squeezed her eyes shut for a brief moment and reopened them a few short seconds later. When she was able to focus, her eyes landed on the Lincoln SUV that pulled up and stopped directly in front of her. Daisy Mae stared at the SUV until the window came down.

"Hey baby, are you alright?" a woman asked her from the driver side of a Lincoln Navigator. Daisy Mae looked at her, and then a smile spread across her lips.

"Yes baby, God has long arms. He done brought me this far," she said, and then she turned away. She turned her back on the lady in the SUV and tightened her grip on her Bible. She proceeded towards the church but paused in her tracks when she heard the woman call out to her again.

"Amen to that," the stranger said and then she pulled off into traffic. Daisy Mae never looked back, but she threw her right hand in the air and added, "God is good. Greater than anyone and everything." She continued on with her side to side limp with the sight of the church building coming into a clearer view.

"Thank you, Jesus!" she mumbled to herself.

As she got closer, she scanned the front of the church and noticed the many different cars that were in the parking lot. The front of the church was made of red brick and there were two women ushers standing outside the white double doors waiting to greet members. That made Daisy Mae feel that much better because she felt that both of the ladies were waiting for her. The church was on the same side of the street that she was already walking on. Moving at a casual pace on the concrete side walk, she'd finally made it to her destination. Before she could make it to the steps of the church she heard, "Sister Daisy." A tall woman walked up to her and then gave her warm embrace.

"Hey baby," Daisy Mae said lovingly and gave her a gentle squeeze. Everything about the lady seemed genuine, from her touch to the warmness that generated from her eyes. The lady that she hugged was known to be a strong God-fearing woman and just like Daisy Mae, she carried her Bible as if it was her weapon of choice. She pulled back from her and they exchanged a momentary gaze.

"Hi are you, Daisy Mae? Is everything going alright? You look tired this morning, and something about the look in your eyes seems to be troubling," Sister Linda said.

Daisy Mae was always a private woman. She never wanted to trouble or worry others, so she hesitated to speak.

"I, I, I, I'm... ummm..." she fumbled.

Sister Linda put her finger up to her lips and cut her off.

"Shhhh... we can talk later," she said, and Daisy Mae was relieved that she didn't push. "You got to go on inside and tend to them children."

Daisy Mae nodded.

"Yes, indeed I do," she said and moved towards the steps that lead to the front entrance of the church.

Daisy Mae was the Sunday school teacher for the youth. The class was made up mostly of teenagers from the ages of twelve to sixteen. Daisy Mae had taught some of the best classes in the last few years. Some of the kids that she had taught years ago had gone to college and got their degrees, got married and now had children of their own.

She was hard on the kids and even herself, but she wanted to make sure that people really got the best out of life. However, there were a few of them that didn't make it out so successful. Two of the younger brothers that came up in the church and attended her classes, wound up going to federal prison on drug and gun charges. Erica, that was Daisy Mae's little sweet heart, she got on crack at the age of fourteen and crushed the entire community. The church knew that Daisy Mae took losing Erica to the streets the hardest, because she spoke highly of her. When they found poor Erica's body in an abandoned house somewhere on the Westside of Atlanta, Daisy Mae was devastated.

Daisy Mae had finally made her way up the steps, she took another deep breath just as both of the ushers greeted her with a firm handshake, then a quick hug and a smile. Finally, she headed on inside the church. When she got inside, she stopped and looked around for a second, she then raised her head and continued on with her signature side to side wobble down the red velvety carpet. Then all of sudden she didn't feel right, but she didn't know what the feeling was, but something washed over her, her stomach tightened up a little, then a small sharp pain pinched the right side of her forehead. She closed her eyes for a second and tried to shake the feeling she was having.

The musicians began to play, and it took Daisy Mae a moment or two to register in her head that the sounds were coming from the organ and piano, that relaxed her a little. She moved her lips silently singing the verse. 'Have you been tried in the fire? Yes.' Feeling like she could continue on, she looked in the area where her class was normally seated, and the four wooden pews were empty. She stopped singing and her eyes instantly went up to the deacon. Something was wrong because when she looked over at him, he shifted his eyes in another direction as if he knew that she was about to ask him something and he wasn't interesting in answering.

She stared at him for a moment and slowly shook her head

side to side. She started to walk again, her name was being called but she didn't bother to look to see who was calling her and she clearly didn't answer. She went through a side door that was on a swinging hinge, the room was much smaller. She stopped in her tracks and looked around, there her class was, sitting in fold out metal chairs that were structured in a half a circle. There were fifteen of them all together and each chair was occupied with boys and girls. They all looked up at her and spoke to her in unison with a simple, "Good morning, Miss Daisy."

She tried her best to give a smile, and then she said, "Good morning." Her tone of voice was dry.

It wasn't because of the kids, but she wanted to know what in the world was going on with the young lady that was sitting in the center of the class as if she was their new teacher or something. Her name was Annabelle, but most of her friends called her Anna or just plain ole Belle. Annabelle was only twenty-one years old and had been a member of the church just a little over six months, her skin was a smooth honey and yellow complexion or somewhere in between, and she was petite but well-shaped. She was dressed in a simple long blue skirt and a loosely fitting turtle neck sweater and leather boots that came up to her calves.

Annabelle had her Bible in her lap, she turned around and looked up at Daisy Mae, giving her the most beautiful smile ever and moved her bible and stood to her feet.

"Good morning, Sister Daisy." Her tone of voice was soft and elegant, but with a powerful authority as the words escaped mouth. Her teeth were white as pearls, but she had had a small gap just in the front of her top teeth that was almost unnoticeable.

Daisy Mae didn't respond right then, something was telling her not to. But in reality, she was in her feelings because someone else was teaching her class. That was her class, and it had been that way for years and she didn't want it any other way. She did everything she could to suppress the negative energy boiling inside of her. She wanted to say what was on her mind, but she held restraint.

"I was just warming the class up for you until you got here," Annabelle said politely. "Please... Have a seat."

Daisy Mae's eyes was locked on Annabelle for a brief moment, and then she scanned the faces of the children. They all looked directly at her as if they wanted answers too. Deciding to deal with Annabelle being there later, she finally removed her jacket. She eased her body around to the metal foldout chair and sat down. She sat her Bible in her lap and flipped it open to

Psalms 120:1. And without telling the class to follow her lead she just started reading.

"I call on the Lord in my distress, and he answers me...," her words trailed off and the entire room fell silent. Annabelle didn't take a seat; she just stood to the far right against the wall watching as if she was observing the way Daisy Mae did things.

Daisy Mae tried to not let Annabelle's presence distract her, so she started over.

"I call on the Lord in my distress, and he answers me...," she recited again. Heavy hearted, her eyes teared up. She tried her best to hold back, but a tear slowly rolled down her right cheek. She repeated the verse again, then again and then over again.

The class was looking at her and from the look on their young faces, she knew they all could tell that something was wrong. Daisy Mae began to rock in her chair, her hands started to shake uncontrollably, then her body jerked as if a jolt of lightning had gone through her. She kicked her legs out and her head and neck turned stiff. Right there in her chair in front of the class, Daisy May had a stroke.

2

*T*he entire church had shut down and an ambulance had arrived about fifteen minutes later. Daisy Mae was lifted upon the stretcher by the two paramedics, her eyes were closed, and she looked sweet but helpless. When she was loaded into the rear of the ambulance, Annabelle hopped into the rear with her. Pastor James was standing there at the back door, he was tall and handsome with a chiseled face and a sculpted beard, his eyes were blood shot-red, but he wasn't crying. There was a concerned look on his face.

He cleared his throat and said, "Annabelle, are you staying at the hospital with her?"

She turned and faced him, and then she nodded her head and said, "Yes." Then she wiped her eyes with a napkin just as one of the paramedics were closing the rear doors. Annabelle looked down at Daisy Mae, she was hooked up to tubes and an IV machine. She couldn't stand to see her like that, it made her stomach tight. Then she reached down and grabbed her left hand, pulled it up to her face and kissed the back of it, and with a low whisper she began to pray.

"Dear Father, never have I been a selfish person in life, nor in

Christ. And I will not start today. My prayer to you today is to keep Miss Daisy safe and strong. I know she's in pain, I know she's hurting and I also know that you're not ready for her yet. Hand me her pain and burdens, any and all struggles and problems that she's having; I'll take them. Please heal her, Father God, protect her..." She wiped her teary eyes and felt her lips begin to nervously shake. Then she went on. "In Jesus' name, Amen."

Then she felt Daisy Mae's hand go limp.

❧

AN HOUR LATER, ANNABELLE WAS INSIDE ONE OF THE WAITING rooms at Grady Memorial Hospital, along with a few more women from the church. They were all standing in a circle holding hands and saying a group prayer for Daisy Mae. Even though the doctors hadn't said anything yet, they all had had strong faith that she was going to be alright. After their prayer ended, they all had a seat except Annabelle, she was the most concerned because deep down inside she felt like she brought everything about for Daisy Mae. One of the ladies looked at her and saw the worry on her face, she walked over to her and gave her a hug. Annabelle's arms went around the lady also and the stranger whispered in her ear.

"It's in God's hands now, baby; don't worry yourself."

Annabelle nodded her head, but her nerves were all over the place.

"I'm trying," was all she managed to say.

She removed herself from the lady's arms and walked out of the waiting room and up the corridor to the nurse's station. There were three nurses there, one of them had her face in a computer and the other two was standing in the rear looking at something on the screen of her iPhone. Annabelle couldn't believe what she was seeing.

"Excuse me," she said loud enough for all three of them to

hear her. They all looked up at her and the lady at the computer responded first.

"Yes, hi may I help you?"

"Can you please tell me the status of Miss Carter?"

The nurse at the computer bunched her eyebrows together as if she didn't have a clue who she was talking about. But just as she was looking at the clipboard, a short Asian doctor was coming around the corner and walked straight up to Annabelle and extended his hand.

"Good morning and good news," he said.

She gripped his hand and her eyes were asking the question before her words came. Then she said, "She's alright?"

"Yes, we're going to keep her for a couple of days to monitor her, she had a light stroke but nothing life threating," he explained.

Annabelle closed her eyes and said, "Thank you, Jesus." Then she asked him, "Can we see her?"

"Yes, maybe just you for now, are you her daughter?" he said and placed his other hand on her shoulder.

Annabelle didn't want to lie but at this point she had no other choice. Just as she was about to say yes, another voice came from behind her and said, "No, she's not; I am."

Annabelle turned around and stared into the eyes of a short chubby woman that was in her mid-fifties wearing a long blond wig with bulging eyes. The woman smelled like stale cigarette smoke.

"Why you looking at me like I'm lying or something?" she barked at Annabelle. She had a funky attitude and the eye rolling was accompanied by neck rolling.

Annabelle didn't even get a chance to respond as the lady nearly pushed her out the way to get around to the doctor.

"Daisy Mae Carter is my mother; do you need to see some driver's licenses or something?" she asked with annoyance.

The doctor eyed her for a moment or two. Annabelle knew

why he took a step back to put some distance between him and the woman, because she reeked of onions, marijuana and cigarettes. He then looked at Annabelle without saying anything and the woman who claimed to be Daisy Mae's daughter continued to rant.

"What the hell you looking at her for? Didn't I say that I was her daughter," she snapped. She was definitely high, drunk and clearly out of control.

Annabelle couldn't believe the way that the woman was acting, and she didn't want any parts of it. She wasn't an aggressive woman or in any mood for a fight, so without saying another word, she turned around and politely walked off. She didn't even bother going back to the waiting room and went straight to the elevator and pressed the number for the first floor. As she waited, there were several things going through her mind as to how she got there in the first place. *I'm just good at doing God's work*, she thought to herself. When the doors parted on the elevator, she stepped inside. She rode down shaking her head at what she had just witnessed with the woman upstairs and wondered if she truly was Daisy Mae's daughter. They had never met, so she wasn't sure if she was telling the truth or not, all she knew was that she didn't want to get into an altercation with the woman. When she got to the lobby, she gave the other sisters an update on Daisy Mae and said the doctor was only allowing immediate family members to visit, so they left. She got outside, and she realized that her car was still at the church, so one of the sisters offered to give her a ride.

No more than an hour later, she was back in the parking lot of the church and got inside of her Honda Accord. By the time she started the engine and was about to put her car in reverse, she noticed the deacon in her review mirror, sitting in his white Mercedes S550, his arm was hanging out the driver's side window waving at her. She left the car running and stepped out and he was also stepping out at the same time. He walked up to her.

"What happened at the hospital?" he asked her with a hint of concern in his voice.

Annabelle took a deep breath.

"I'm not sure, I was on the way to the back to go see Miss Daisy Mae and this rude lady approached the doctor and I claiming to be Daisy Mae's daughter. Since I'm not immediate family that canceled out my visit with her. The doctor did say she was doing good and it was not life threatening."

"Good, good," he said and placed his hand on her shoulder.

"Well, it sounds like the lady that came up there was her daughter, Pearl; she could be a real pain at times. Everybody knows her and how she treats her mama, but Sister Daisy don't like people in her business so the church kind of like stayed out of her personal business and issues with Pearl."

"Well, I can definitely see why Daisy Mae doesn't talk about her much, because she has never told me about Pearl."

"Nine times out of ten that is the reason. Pearl doesn't have it all upstairs..." he held up his hands and said.

"Lord forgive me, but I'm speaking the truth." He shook his head and tried to keep himself from laughing and when Annabelle noticed his smirk, she started smiling also and then they both started laughing. Annabelle caught herself and covered her mouth. The deacon whose name was Charles said, "Did she really go up into that hospital acting a fool?"

"Yes, but I definitely wasn't about to stay there and argue with her crazy behind. I just honestly, I wanted to make sure that Sister Daisy was fine."

Charles looked at his watch, and she could see it read ten after one. Then his eyes went back to Annabelle.

"I'm going to need a small favor from you," he said.

Her stare was now on him with eagerness. She was inclined to hear what he had to say. "I'm listening," she finally said.

"Hi do you feel about being the head Sunday school teacher for the church until sister Daisy gets well?"

Annabelle shrugged her shoulders lightly and said, "If it's not a problem and the church..."

"The church wants you in that position, the kids love you. I'm sure you'll do fine," he assured her. Then he took a deep breath and went on, "Our church is growing, and you should grow with us."

"I don't have a problem with that, but what if I get in good and sister Daisy wants her position back?"

"Let the Mother's board handle that part," he said. "I have another position for sister Daisy." Then he extended his hand and she shook it.

"Thank you," she said.

He nodded his head with a smile. "No problem, I'll see you in a couple of days, okay." He turned around and hopped in the driver's side of his S550 and slowly pulled off. Annabelle got into her car and did the same thing and headed home.

Home for Annabelle at that time was a shelter for women in Atlanta. She didn't have plans on living there forever but definitely until she got herself together. Once inside, she went straight to the room she lived in and shared with three other women. She wasn't anti-social, but Annabelle didn't talk too much. She mainly stayed in her Bible, studying the word and taking notes. That day she was a little tired, and hungry but she had faith that everything was going to be alright soon and things would get better. She sat down on her bed and rubbed her hands over her face and thought back to how she'd actually got there.

Just only two years ago, Annabelle was living in a two-bedroom house in Augusta, Georgia, the city that she was born and raised in. She lived in a small A-frame house made of wood and aluminum siding with her auntie Kim, her mother's one and only baby sister. However, Kim was more like an older sister instead of an auntie to her. Annabelle had had big dreams and hopes of becoming a doctor when she was at Laney High School until her mother died of cancer. Things then changed for Annabelle and she had a mental breakdown. She went into a shell and stopped enjoying life and being around folks.

She started questioning God every day with the question of why, but she got no answers. She didn't have a clue why He'd take her mother away and just didn't understand it. She went from being one of the most popular girls in school to getting bullied and teased. They'd call her crazy and picked on her just because she was always quiet and to herself. She did have a few friends that stuck with her along her journey, but Annabelle had shut down on them also and separated herself from the world. After she graduated from high school, she started taking free online Bible courses because she was still seeking questions from God as to why her mother was taken away from her so soon. Nothing ever came about from it, but she never stopped praying about it. Soon after graduation, she'd gotten herself a decent job working at a meat packing slaughter house called FPL.

Her second day on the job, she quit. When she got to her auntie's house in the middle of the day, it was loud music playing when she entered the living room, the smell of loud marijuana was thick in the air, and in the middle of the floor was her auntie Kim, naked with two men having sex. She couldn't believe her eyes and when Kim noticed her standing there she said, "You can stand there and watch, or you can join in."

One of the guys was tall and dark, he looked back at her with big buck eyes and examined her up and down.

"I can make her join in," the man said as he continued to eye Annabelle like she was a piece of meat.

Before another word was said, Annabelle quickly turned around and ran out the door and only returned to get her personal belongings one day when the house was empty. The following day, she got her a one-way bus ticket to Atlanta and never looked back. She never questioned her decision of abruptly leaving, all she knew was that she didn't want any parts of a lifestyle like her auntie Kim had. Later, she did contact her auntie to let her know that she was alright but not one time did she tell anybody where she was at.

She shook off the horrible memories of her past. Just the thought of being raped always terrified Annabelle. She got down on her knees, pressed her hands together to make the perfect praying hands and she began praying silently for Sister Daisy Mae. Annabelle was strong in her faith, she knew God wouldn't let her down. Even if things didn't go exactly as she wanted, she trusted in God enough to know He'd bring her through any situation. That's how she was feeling deep down inside because He had brought her through some troubling times.

A woman's voice from behind made her open her eyes.

"I feel you, baby; pray yo' way up outta this damn shelter. And while you at it, say one for me too because I'm damn sho' bout to go take this hot credit card up in Macy's to get my baby some clothes," she added.

Annoyed by the interruption, Annabelle rolled her eyes, and then finally looked back at her standing in her doorway. She was one of the ladies that also lived there, and she wasn't one of Annabelle's favorites.

"You need some clothes, some underwear or something?" she offered.

"No, thanks, and I'll definitely say a prayer for you." Annabelle stood and moved in her direction and outstretched her hands.

"Oh, you dead serious? I just meant when you pray, not right now," she said.

Annabelle still waited for her to give her her hands. Finally, she did, and Annabelle received them with a gentle squeeze.

"Now close your eyes and bow your head," Annabelle instructed, and she obliged.

"Dear Father, I come to you in prayer this day to ask you to cover this young lady with nothing but great energy, protect her, cover her with your precious blood and let her make it back here safe today. In Jesus name we pray. Amen."

"Amen," the girl said, lifted her head with her eyes open and looked Annabelle in the eyes.

"Aye, I really felt that. You got some powerful words inside of you, giiiiirrrrrrllllllll," she dragged. "Got a bish ready to go get saved and all."

"Let me know when you ready to change your life. I have a great church home, and we'd welcome you with open arms."

"I don't know about all that. It be some mad crazy things going on in churches these days."

"That depends on what you looking for. Some people come for the wrong reasons. And when you have the wrong energy, you attract the wrong energy as well."

"I know that's right, cause I'll probably be trying to sale baby clothes and food stamp cards and Lord knows what else." she joked, laughing lightly at herself. Then she said, "Listen, my name is Angel, but I go by Black Girl in these streets though and right now, I gotta go handle my business."

"Okay, Angel," Annabelle said with a smile. "With a name like that, I'm sure it's a reason behind it. We'll talk about it more later." Annabelle let her hands go and she turned and walked away. Annabelle looked at her as she made her way down the hallway. Putting her prayer plans on hold for the time being, she left her room and walked outside to the front of the shelter. She shoved her hands into her pockets and paced the pavement for a few moments, and then she headed to the rear of the shelter for a little more peace. She took a seat in one the chairs in the serenity area. Annabelle just looked around, lost in her own thoughts for a moment.

She began thinking about her new position at the church as the new Sunday school teacher. That was great news to her, but she was still wondering about taking Daisy Mae's place. Filling in was one thing, but taking her spot was something unsettling, so she knew she had to pray on it more. Although she had agreed with the deacon to do it, she needed confirmation from God to move forward with becoming the permanent teacher.

She was worried, if Daisy Mae would recover well enough to even take her position back. More issues about her life danced around in her head, but she then thought of the well-being of sister Daisy Mae and if what she was doing was okay.

"I got to go back to this hospital," she said and stood up.

She knew she'd be unable to rest easy until she found out the real status of her situation. As she walked back inside to gather her things, she noticed that her phone wasn't where she had just left it. She looked around the room, and then she noticed one of the ladies sitting over across the room at a round plastic table playing solitaire with a worn-down deck of cards. Annabelle casually walked over to the table and sat down across from her and just sat there and stared at the lady until she finally looked up and asked, "Why you looking at me?"

Annabelle had to keep a straight face after seeing that this mysterious woman was missing her top four front teeth.

"I just wanted to know if you saw anyone take my phone from my bed?" Annabelle asked.

"Ask God, you ask him for everything else. I'm sure he'll tell you." She laughed loudly.

Annabelle couldn't even believe what she said, that made her stare at her for a long moment until her eyes teared up. The strange woman went back to playing solitaire as if nothing had happened. She finally wiped her eyes with the back of her hand and stood up. Before she left the room, she whispered, "Thank you anyway, and I'm sorry for bothering you."

$\mathcal{B}$y the time Annabelle made it back to the hospital and upstairs to Daisy Mae's room her crazy daughter was gone. When she walked inside the room, she noticed Daisy Mae was lying up in her bed with an IV tube wedged in her arm. She was sleeping peacefully as could be. Annabelle walked up beside her and gently rubbed the side of her face with the back her of her hand and whispered, "I'm here sister, this Annabelle." Then she began smoothing her hair to the back with her hand until Daisy Mae finally opened her eyes.

"Hey baby." Her voice was low and weak. The look in her eyes assured Annabelle that Daisy Mae was happy to see her.

Annabelle smiled, leaned in and kissed the side of her face.

"Hi are you feeling?"

"Pretty good I guess. I am ready to go home, and I am hungry."

Annabelle smiled down at her.

"I'm not sure how long the doctors want to keep you, but we'll definitely know something by in the morning."

"Are you gonna stay all night with me?" Daisy Mae asked

Annabelle, her voice was low as a whisper, but Annabelle heard her.

"I'm not sure if I can stay all night, but I will definitely see if I can. I'm not sure if you know your daughter came to see you. I don't think that she wanted me to see you earlier today."

"I am aware that she came, the nurse told me and told me how she showed her behind. To keep security from coming, she left. I got a feeling she won't be back, so I'll let the doctor know that I need you here with me. I don't believe that it will be a problem."

That warmed Annabelle's heart to hear that from Daisy Mae and she had no problems with staying with her. A huge smile plastered across her face.

"Well, if it's not a problem, I'll stay tonight and as many nights as you'd like until you're released." She reached down and grabbed Daisy Mae's hand, and in a jokingly manner she said, "Now, I don't want your daughter coming up in here trying to put a beat down on me."

"No honey, all she wanted to know was if I was dead, so she could get some money from the insurance policy. When she came in I pretended to be asleep. I overheard her fussing with them nurses and then she had the nerve to ask the nurse to hook her up with some Percocet pain pills promising her that she would make sure she cut her in on the profits. But I know better. Even if the nurse was fool enough to fall for that bunch of bull, that heffa would have run up out of here faster than an Olympic track star to take them herself."

Annabelle chuckled a little bit, because from the looks and reeking scent that Pearl gave off, she doubted she sold any drugs that came into her possession. She took a seat and just sat there listening and shaking her head at the same time to some of the stories Daisy Mae had shared with her about her daughter. There chit-chats were interrupted by a light tap on the door. The same doctor from earlier entered Daisy Mae's room, and when he saw Annabelle he smiled at her.

"Hey, glad you made it back," he said to her.

Annabelle flashed him a smile. "I'm glad to be back doctor. I had to check on our patient."

The doctor turned his attention to Daisy Mae.

"Hi are you feeling?" he asked her, with the tone of a concerned physician.

"I'm doing better doctor and I'm really ready to go home. Can I leave today?"

The doctor smiled. "Not today Miss Carter. We want to keep you at least forty- eight hours. I can't just let you up and leave like that and you're not well enough, so in a couple of days we'll see how you're doing."

"But I feel well doc," Daisy Mae replied. "And I want me some Ox tails, rice, cabbage, cornbread and gravy. Not this nasty hospital food. My dinner is at home just waiting for me to return."

"In that case, I'm definitely not letting you go home, Miss Carter. You can't consume anything like that and I don't recommend that you do so for a while, so although it's not your meal of choice, you're going to have to stay and eat what the dietitian says."

Daisy Mae's expression was of someone defeated, so she didn't make any more fuss. She let out a breath and said, "Well, if you are going to keep me in this place, I need Annabelle to stay overnight with me if it's alright."

The doctor looked over at Annabelle with a questioning look.

"Normally, overnight stays are for immediate family only and your daughter didn't seem too pleased with Annabelle earlier. If she comes back, and things get crazy, we'll have to call security again. Are you sure you want that type of conflict?" he asked.

Annabelle spoke up first. "I'm sure, I can handle myself."

Then Daisy Mae said, "Oh, she gonna be alright. God is all

over this room sweetheart and there is no weapon form against saints," she added.

The doctor nodded and then got Daisy Mae's chart. He read all of her vitals and numbers and wrote down a few notes. He then turned his attention back to Daisy Mae.

"I'll be here first thing in the morning to check on you. You rest and take it easy," he said and patted the back of her hand.

"I will, doctor."

"And no feeding my patient soul food. Right now, we need a good diet."

"I understand," Annabelle said. When he walked out the door, she turned to Daisy Mae. "Now, you heard what the doctor said and he's right. I can run to the store and get you something to eat. Maybe some fruit and steamed veggies, but no Oxtails for you."

Daisy Mae looked at Annabelle with a displeasing stare.

"I thought you wanted to help me out, fruit and steamed vegetables? You're going to starve me."

Annabelle reached over and ran her hand down the side of her cheek.

"You got to trust me on this one, because we're definitely going to have to switch your diet Daisy Mae," she admonished. Then she reached in her pocket to pull out her cellphone and realized that it wasn't there, her facial expression changed.

"What's wrong?" she asked her. Her eyes were searching Annabelle's face for questions.

Annabelle didn't want to put Daisy Mae in her business and at the same time she didn't want to lie to her either, so she said, "I forgot that I misplaced my phone."

"Where were you when you lost it?"

Oh God, she thought to herself, because she didn't want to have this conversation about her living situation. She didn't want the members of her church to know she was living in a shelter. At least not right now anyway. Annabelle was quiet and still for a moment with her eyes roaming around the room as if she expected the walls to give her answers to the question Daisy Mae had asked. She then waved her hand in the air to dismiss what Daisy Mae had asked.

"Let me go get your food, you got to be starving," she said, trying to hurry out of the room.

Daisy Mae's voice caused her to halt. "Annabelle," Daisy Mae called out like a mother. "Tell me what's going on, Annabelle," she said, that time raising her raspy tone.

Annabelle took a deep breath, turned back to Daisy Mae and her eyes went straight to hers. She let out a deep breath and told the truth about her living arrangements.

"I live in a women's shelter here in Atlanta. When I went back after trying to visit with you earlier, I put my things down and walked outside for a little while. When I went back inside, my phone was missing. I asked one of the ladies that I share the room with did she see anybody get it and she went left field on me, so I just left and came here," she said and let out a small breath.

"And hi long have you been living in a shelter?" Daisy Mae asked her with a voice of concern, her eyes fixed on Annabelle and darting side to side.

"Off and on for about eighteen months, at different ones though." That took a lot out of her because she was really private, and she had never actually shared that information with anyone.

"Do you work?" Daisy Mae asked her.

"I was working as an Uber driver for a little while, then..." she paused. She could feel the tears welling in her eyes, but she swallowed hard and blinked back the tears. Daisy Mae motioned for her to come back and have a seat and she went over and eased down into the chair.

"I understand, baby," Daisy May said tenderly. "Life is hell, excuse my language. Especially here in Atlanta. You got to be careful."

Annabelle nodded. "I know."

"And where you from?" Daisy Mae asked her.

"Originally from Augusta," she sniffled and then wiped her eyes.

"Baby, you got to stop all this cryin' now, cause you gonna make me cry. Seems like you've been praying so hard for other people that you've been forgetting to pray for yourself. But it happens like that sometimes, and all this here happened for a reason. We should never question God." She moved both of her hands in a circular motion.

"He's working right now in this hospital room, not just for me, but for you also, okay?"

Annabelle nodded her head.

"I know. And I believe," she said. She talked with Daisy Mae a few more minutes and then offered again to go and get her something to eat. Daisy Mae declined and was soon fast asleep.

The following morning, Annabelle was in the hospital bathroom brushing her teeth. After she rinsed and wiped her mouth, she just stood there in the mirror for a moment. She stared in her own eyes and she had to admit to herself that she looked tired and drained. She knew that she wasn't getting the proper amount of rest and now it was beginning to show. All she could do was shake her head at herself and remind herself that she'd do better.

She turned off the water, dried her hands and then she walked out of the bathroom. Not happy to see Daisy Mae slowly standing up on her own, she asked, "What are you doing?"

She smiled. "I'm feeling better, and I'm in no pain whatsoever, so I think we'll be leaving here today."

"Now, Sister Daisy, you know we got to follow the doctor's orders and he didn't say anything about you leaving today. Like I told you, I'm going to stay here with you until he says you're clear. You can't diagnose yourself and I say we wait to hear the word from your doctor."

Daisy Mae let out a huff and then walked in Annabelle's direction.

"Well fine. Okay, baby, I'm going to the bathroom."

Annabelle stepped aside and watched as Daisy Mae walk in her same side to side motion to make it to the bathroom. Once she was inside with the door closed, Annabelle walked over to the window and opened the curtain to let in the sun light. The room got bright instantly, and Annabelle looked up at the sky. It was pretty outside, and the sun was shining so brightly. The sky was a deep blue and the milky white clouds were slowly cruising by. Annabelle admired the scenery before her mind went back to the position they had given her at the church as the head Sunday school teacher. She was grateful for the offer and wanted to do the Lord's work, but she still was uneasy and knew that she couldn't keep that information from Daisy Mae. She was contemplating on how she was going to tell her. Then she thought, *it can't be that hard. I've told this lady everything about me.*

She heard the toilet flush, then the water running in the sink. Annabelle turned around when Daisy Mae was coming out of the bathroom. Before Annabelle could say anything, Daisy Mae said to her, "Will you take my place for me at the church until I'm ready to go back to teaching?"

Annabelle rushed over to help her back into the bed before she answered.

"I am glad that you asked, because I was meaning to talk to you about it. Yesterday, when I went back for my car, Deacon Charles asked if I could," she said, but the knock on the door interrupted her mid-sentence.

A young and pretty pecan tan nurse walked in with a plastic breakfast tray.

"Good morning, Miss Carter, I have your breakfast."

"Baby, you can take it back with you. My niece was just about to go get us some breakfast," Daisy Mae quickly said with a slight frown.

The nurse looked at her.

"Are you sure?" Then her eyes went to Annabelle.

Annabelle nodded her head and the nurse smiled and turned around and left the room. Just as she was walking out of the door, in came a short stocky guy with dreads. He had a mouth full of gold teeth, a thick gold chain was hanging around his neck and he carried a big pink teddy bear and some flowers. When he saw Daisy Mae, he walked over to her with a smile. He put the flowers and bear down and then leaned in and gave her a hug.

"Hey grandma," he said, and then he kissed her cheek.

"Look like you doin' good to me. Hi you feelin'?" he pulled back from her.

"I'm doing good, baby; ready to leave now," Daisy Mae said.

"That's good to hear," he said to her and then he turned and looked at Annabelle.

"And who is this young beautiful lady right here, grandma?" he asked with his eyes moving up and down her body.

"Her name is, Annabelle. Annabelle, this is Deon, he is a member of the church; he was one of the students in my Sunday school class years ago," she said.

Annabelle extended his hand out to him and he shook it and held on to it for a brief moment. "Nice to meet you, Annabelle."

"Nice to meet you, too. Are you still active at the church?" she asked him because she didn't recognize him at all.

He smiled and said. "Nah, I got sidetracked a little bit but I'm coming back soon."

Daisy Mae butted in.

"His butt out there running them streets that's why he ain't been coming. But that's another story I guess." She rolled her eyes in a playful manner and Deon went and put his arm around her neck.

"Don't do me like that, grandma." He looked at Annabelle and said, "I'm really in the music industry, but she think I'm out here messing around."

Annabelle didn't know how to respond to that, so she turned to Daisy Mae.

"Listen, I'm going to run out and get you some breakfast."

"I can go get breakfast, what y'all want?" Deon offered.

"Maybe Waffle House," Annabelle said, and then looked at Daisy Mae.

"Chicken breast, eggs, toast and orange juice."

"That sounds good to me," Daisy Mae agreed. She then waved Deon to come in closer. He leaned into and she whispered something in his ear.

He nodded his head. "No problem," he answered and then he reached in his front right pocket and pulled out a knot of hundred-dollar bills, unfolded them and counted off thirty of them and handed the money to Daisy Mae.

"I'm about to go get the food and I'll be back in a few." He turned and left.

When he walked out the door Daisy Mae reached for Annabelle's hand, and when she put her hand in Daisy Mae's, she put the money in hers.

"Go get you a new phone and go get yourself a place. I don't want you in that shelter after this week." She squeezed her hand to let her know she was dead serious.

"Sister Daisy... I can't, I can't take this," she tried to say.

Daisy Mae's head shook side to side.

"You can, and you will. I'm your elder, don't go against what God has planned for you, okay? Now, take this money and do as I say," she ordered.

Annabelle leaned in and wrapped her arms around Daisy Mae's neck and just held her for a long moment. Then she whispered in her ear, "I can't even thank you enough."

"You don't have to thank me, baby. This is all God's plan."

Annabelle was sincerely grateful and in no position not to accept the help. By four thirty that same evening, Annabelle was brushing Daisy Mae's hair. She'd already helped her wash up in the tub and when she came back from getting her phone, she also brought back a few things from Walmart for herself and Daisy Mae. That night they ate chicken salad from Zaxbys and the following morning Daisy Mae was checking out of Grady hospital. Annabelle was there the entire time with her. She took Daisy Mae home in her car. Daisy Mae lived on a quiet street in a green wooden house with a screened in front porch. The front yard was a mixture of red dirt and green grass. Annabelle pulled in the driveway and switched off the engine. When she got out, she walked around and opened the door for Daisy Mae and placed her hand on her arm to assist her in getting out the car.

"I'm alright, baby," she said and swung her legs out of the car before Annabelle lifted her to help her stand. Annabelle closed the door for her as Daisy Mae walked toward the house. Annabelle then opened the back door and grabbed her flowers, teddy bear, and bags and followed her inside the house.

When Daisy Mae got in the front living room she turned on the lights. Annabelle noticed the hardwood floors that framed the area rug in the center beneath the glass coffee table. The room was furnished with a three-piece leather sofa set that looked plush and comfortable. Annabelle admired the décor but didn't expect something so modern in a home of a woman that was Daisy Mae's age.

"Have a seat, baby," Daisy Mae suggested. "Please make yourself at home."

Annabelle sat all of Daisy Mae belongings down on the nearby sofa and then grabbed a seat on the couch. She looked around at all the pictures on the wall and then she stood up and walked across the room to get a closer look at one of them. The first person she spotted was Daisy Mae on the second row of women in front of the church. She was much younger in the picture, and she looked sophisticated. She turned to Daisy Mae.

"You were young on this picture, and jazzy," she added.

Daisy Mae walked over to where she was standing and examined the same picture.

"Yes, I was, maybe thirty-five or so. That photo was taken back in the early eighties. I was a member of the usher board and that there," she said, giving a point. "That was my best friend, Tootie. The Lord called her home some years ago and that one right there is Miss Cook. She went on to glory after a heart attack five years ago." Daisy Mae leaned in a little closer for a closer examination and then continued, "Now, this is Helen," she paused for a moment a two.

"Did she die, too?" Annabelle asked.

"No, but I haven't seen her in a long spell. I mean this picture right her brings back some old memories."

"I can imagine," Annabelle said.

Daisy Mae looked at her and nodded with agreement.

"Come and follow me," she said and started towards the kitchen. They walked until they stopped at a wooden door. Daisy Mae turned the knob to open the door and then she hit the light switch. Inside was a queen-sized bed that looked like it was plush and comfortable. It was made up with a floral duvet and had a spread of colorful pillows across the top. A wooden chair sat in the right corner of the room and the window had lavender colored curtains that matched the bed spread. Daisy Mae turned around and faced Annabelle.

"This is your room until you get on your feet or until you get tired of me nagging," she joked with a light laugh.

Annabelle just stood there speechless at first and then she smiled.

"Thank you," she said and looked around the room. The room was large and beautiful and most importantly, it was quiet and peaceful. Annabelle knew she'd be comfortable there, but instantly she thought of Daisy Mae's daughter. She didn't know if she lived there or not and she didn't want any drama whatsoever.

"I'd love to stay, Sister Daisy, but I just don't want any conflict with your daughter."

"Don't worry about my daughter, Annabelle. This is my home, so you just go and gather your things and come back," she said and then she turned to walk out of the room. She headed towards her bedroom, Annabelle assumed. Annabelle looked around to take it all in, and she let out a sigh and then lifted her arms to give God some praise. She silently thanked him and wiped her tears. She touched the bed and a moment later, Daisy Mae walked back in.

"This is yours, she said and then placed a key into her hand.

Annabelle hugged her so tight.

"I don't know how to repay you for this," she cried.

Daisy Mae patted her back and whispered, "God brought you here, baby. He always protects his Angels."

4

When Annabelle made it back to the shelter, she paused and looked around at the faces of the women who resided there. Many looked sad, while others looked exhausted and defeated. A middle-aged woman sat in the corner, breastfeeding her baby with blood shot red eyes and she looked beyond tired. Annabelle dug into her pocket, retrieved one of the hundreds that she had been blessed with and walked over to her. She handed it to her and the woman quickly swiped it from her hand.

"Thank you, thank you, thank you," the woman repeated.

"You are welcome, and God bless you," Annabelle said and headed up to her room with a smile graced across her face. As soon as she made it inside of her room, she started packing her things inside of a suitcase. She saw the lady that she felt had stolen her cellphone sitting in the corner looking at her with a menacing glare, but Annabelle combatted her ominous look with a smirk and went back to gathering her things. She didn't have much, so not even an hour later, she opened the trunk and begin loading everything.

"Girl, where you been? I've been looking for you for two whole days." The voice from behind her blared.

Annabelle turned around and saw Angel standing there.

"Hey," she said to her. "I'm leaving this place and I'm going to be staying with a friend for a little while."

"What?" Angel said.

"Well, at least let me give you what I got for you before you take off. Stay right here." She turned around and jogged back inside. Annabelle watched her for a brief moment and turned back to the trunk and arranged the suitcase and clothes that were on the clothes hangers. Angel came right back outside carrying a Macys shopping bag and handed it to her.

"I know you said you were good, but I got you some cosmetics, underwear, soaps, oils, body washes and perfume, you know, things that women need," she giggled. Annabelle took the bag and hugged her.

"Thank you, Angel. You didn't have to do this for me."

Then she squeezed her back.

"I did, and you are welcome. You be safe out there, girl, because the struggle is most defiantly real out here."

"Indeed," she agreed and then released her.

"And I really appreciate your prayers and support."

"I really appreciate this as well and maybe one day we'll cross paths again, God willing," Annabelle said. She added the bag that Angel had given her and then closed the trunk. They said their final goodbyes and Annabelle walked around to the driver's side door and opened it. Angel was still standing there watching her leave.

"Stay blessed," Annabelle said and then got into her car and started the engine. When she pulled off, Angel turned and made her way back inside the shelter.

When Annabelle got back to Daisy Mae's house it was late and she didn't want to wake her up. She eased inside the house with her clothes and went straight to her room and unpacked what she had. Afterwards, she went in the bathroom and took herself a long hot shower. The water refreshed her, and it made her feel so good. She was using some of the body wash that Angel had gotten for her. When she dried off, she slipped on her night gown and climbed into bed. She felt her body about to shut down, but she forgot something, so she got back up and got on her knees on the side of the bed and prayed long and hard until she fell asleep right there on the side of the bed in her praying position.

✺

THE FOLLOWING MORNING, DAISY MAE WAS UP BRIGHT AND EARLY sitting at the kitchen table nursing a cup of steaming coffee. She looked up when Annabelle came to the door.

"Good morning," Annabelle said and then took a seat across from her.

"Good morning, Annabelle! Did you sleep well last night?" Daisy Mae asked. She stood up from her chair, went over to the counter and poured Annabelle a cup of coffee. She placed it on the table in front of her and then returned to her chair.

"Thank you for the coffee, and I slept too good last night. It's been a while since I've had that much peace and quiet and a bed so comfortable to rest my body in." She blew into the hot cup to cool down the coffee after she added a little cream and sugar that sat on the table and then she took a small sip, brought the cup down and sipped it again.

"I am so grateful, and I thank you for allowing me to stay in your home. I didn't think I'd end up in a shelter. When I first moved to Atlanta I just wanted to get away from my old life, escape my past and just start over." She paused and then a few seconds later she started again, "My mother was my life, but she was called by God and I didn't have a clue as to why it happened to her so young. She was like the best mother a child could have and I hate cancer took her away. I know I'm not supposed to swear, but that is the strongest word I can think of to express my promise to help save women from dying from it. I can see it, I can feel it. That is a mission for me."

Daisy Mae just sat and listened, looking at the hurt on Annabelle's face made her sad, but she knew what life was all about and with joy, we all experienced pain, something none of us could control.

"The Good Book says, 'Blessed are they that mourn: for they shall be comforted'," Daisy Mae said.

Annabelle smiled. "Matthew chapter five, verse four."

Daisy Mae nodded her head, impressed at the young lady. Then she asked her, "Do you remember what Revelations twenty-one, verse four says?"

"And God shall wipe away all tears from their eyes; and there shall be no more death, neither sorrow, nor crying, neither shall there be any more pain; for the former things are passed away."

Daisy Mae reached across the table with both hands and Annabelle took her hands and they both bowed their heads and Daisy Mae began her prayer.

"There will be many times in our life when we face challenges, hardship, loss, loneliness, and doubt. But the Bible reminds us that God is for us and He works all things together for good and not evil. The Lord Jesus Christ got you covered, baby. You may not be able to see it now, but he has something very special in store for you. All you have to do is have faith and trust and believe in Him."

Annabelle continued to keep her head bowed and her eyes shut.

"I believe in you, Father," she prayed and continued to lay her cares on Christ for a few more moments.

"In Jesus name," she ended and wiped her eyes. She let out a deep breath and then she got up from her seat and walked around the table and gave Daisy Mae a warm hug.

"Thank you for everything."

"You don't owe me a thank you, baby. I'm just doing what I was sent here for."

"I know you are, but I need you to know that you've been a blessing to me and I will never forget it."

"The pleasure is all mine. Now, sit and let me fix you some breakfast," Daisy Mae insisted, and Annabelle didn't dispute. She and Annabelle chatted while Daisy Mae whipped them up some eggs, bacon and biscuits. They ate and then Daisy Mae went back to her room.

Annabelle went to her room to find something to wear before heading out to the church. When Annabelle left the house, she drove straight to her destination. She pulled her car into the parking lot, found a space up front and got out. She'd dressed in a pair of pants, long sleeved top and two-inch heels with a leather jacket. She walked inside of the church, and oddly it was empty, except for a couple of people. She headed to the rear of the church where the offices were. She stopped at the door that read PASTOR on it and she knocked softly.

"Come in." She heard his baritone voice say from the other side of the door.

Annabelle turned the knob and pushed the door open, and the pastor was sitting behind a cherry oak wood desk. He looked up at Annabelle as soon as she stepped inside.

"Hello, Annabelle! Hi you doing, today?" he asked cheerfully.

The Pastor was a smooth looking man, brown skin with thick eyebrows and neatly trimmed beard. He had a strong jawline and thick neck. Annabelle would bet the fragrance he wore was Bond No. 9 because she was familiar with that scent. It had his entire office smelling lovely and she allowed the aroma to tickle her nose before she replied.

"I'm fine, sir. I just wanted to stop by to let you know that

Sister Daisy is well and she's home. I'm staying with her for a few days, so I'll definitely be making sure that she's well taken care of."

"That is great to hear, Annabelle," he responded back, placing his elbows on the desk.

"Great and I also wanted to let you know as far as me being the Sunday school teacher permanently. I want you know that I'm available for it and I'll do whatever service for our church that will help us grow as a whole and move forward."

The pastor stood to his feet and extended his hand out to her and she grabbed it. His grip was strong and powerful.

"Welcome aboard and I really want you to know that the congregation really welcomes you and appreciates you. Let me know if you need anything."

Annabelle let his hand go, and then she said, "I do have a few questions for you, now, if it's okay?"

"Sure, I have a few minutes."

"Well, first, I need to ask you about trips. What do you think about having trips for the youth class? Something like going to a Falcons game or the Georgia Aquarium. Outings and activities are very important, and I can find some ways to keep the cost low and affordable."

"I definitely like the sound of that, see you're starting off on the right page, bringing something different to the table. Our young people are very important to us and we want to keep their young minds focused on God and doing the right thing. Positive enforcements by any means is welcomed and, I'll talk with the mother's board about this later today, so you'll be hearing from me sometime later this evening if that's fine." He pulled out his cellphone. "What's your number?" he asked her.

She nodded and recited the digits as he keyed them into his phone. When he finished punching her number in he looked up at her.

"Great, be looking for my call later."

"Thats fine, sir and thank you," she said and then turned to vacate his office. She closed the door softly behind her and headed back towards the sanctuary. Before she could open the double doors, her cellphone rang out, so she dug into her purse to retrieve it. It was Daisy Mae and she quickly answered.

"Yes, Sister Daisy Mae," she said nervously. She hoped nothing had gone wrong since she left.

"Annabelle, before you come home can you please pick up some cranberry juice? I forgot to get it yesterday while we were out."

Annabelle let out a breath of relief.

"No problem. I should be there soon." She ended the call and dropped her phone back into her purse.

"Thank you, God. Please no more bad news," she said out loud and proceeded into the sanctuary.

§.

AFTER ANNABELLE CLOSED THE DOOR, PASTOR JAMES SAT DOWN and dialed a number on his cellphone and pressed the speaker button. The line rang five times before someone answered.

"Aye, why you calling me this time of the day?" the deep groggy voice asked from the other end.

The Pastor looked at the phone and shook his head. It was his younger brother on the other end and bad as he hated to call him about a financial situation, there he was again.

"Hey, lil brother! Hi you doing?" he asked.

"Oh, so now we back cool again? Man, I tell you the truth, I swear since you been on this preacher church thing you just ain't the same."

"What time can we meet up? I need to speak with you about something," Pastor said ignoring his last statement.

"James, listen at me, bro'. I know you trying to get yourself situated with the church and everything. Financially wise, just let me know what you need because if we meet up you gonna be trying to make me get baptized and saved and all that good stuff, and honestly, I'm not ready for it yet."

James put his hand on his forehead and looked up toward the ceiling while his brother continued to talk.

"You feel where I'm coming from?"

"It's not where you coming from, it's about where you going, Jamal," he finally said when his brother stopped rambling about not being ready to give his life to Christ.

"Yeah, whatever man. Just give me a roundabout figure because I know you need something."

"Yes, I do. But, it's what I need to get for the church. I really need something like a sixteen-passenger sprinter van."

"That's not a problem; I think it's one of them on the car lot. Now, let me know what I need to write the check for."

"Twenty-thousand and make it out to the church."

"Yeah, yeah, make it sound just that easy," Jamal joked.

"One last thing and please just consider it."

"What is it?"

"Come to service on Sunday. I want to let the congregation know who the van and the large check came from. You know I want to give you recognition for your generous gifts."

"Brah, I'm not coming to church. No way, no how. I can be anonymous. I don't need a pat on the back, so Sunday service is a hell to the naw!"

James sat silent on the other line without saying anything. He just held the phone until Jamal gave in.

"Fine! I'll come aw'ight. I'll be there," he finally said and then he ended the call.

On that Sunday morning, Pastor James walked in to see that Annabelle was one of the first people at the church. She was already inside setting up the chairs for the class. That Sunday, she was dressed in a long khaki skirt and a white long sleeve blouse and two-inch ankle boots. He watched as she removed

Bibles from a cardboard box and she placed one in each chair. From where he was standing, he could see that they were new. They were leatherback with gold embossed letters and he wondered why she didn't tell him that the children needed new bibles. He certainly didn't want her to be burdened with the churches expenses, so he made a mental note to ask her the price, so he could reimburse her.

"Good morning, Annabelle, sorry to bother you," he interrupted her.

"Good morning, Pastor, hi is everything?"

"Everything is wonderful," he said and put his hands upon his waist.

"Great to hear." She smiled.

"Listen, I know you are preparing for your Sunday school class, but I need a favor from you."

"Sure Pastor, it's okay. What is it?" she inquired.

"Will you ride with me to my brother's place to pick up our new sprinter van? I thought about what you said about the trips for the kids and it will also be a good way for us to pick up our members that don't have any transportation."

"Sure, do you think we'll be back before my class starts?"

James flipped his wrist and looked at his watch, it was eight o'clock a.m. He glanced back at her. "I'm sure we will, if we head out now."

"That's cool, let me grab my purse," she said.

After she threw her strap over her shoulder, she followed Pastor James outside to a glossy black Cadillac SUV. She went around to the passenger side and he hopped in the driver seat and started the engine. When Annabelle closed the door and strapped herself behind the seatbelt, she looked at him and said, "This is nice."

"Thanks," he said and then backed out of the parking space. They pulled out of the parking lot and got onto the main road. A few short minutes later, they were out in traffic and emerging out on to I-20 East. James was doing eighty miles per hour trying to get to his destination. They rode in silence for a long minute. Annabelle was staring out the passenger side window, looking at the passing cars that they seemed to be flying by. Then no more than ten minutes later, they were exiting from the I-20 expressway and heading downtown.

Pastor James took a few turns here and there until he pulled up into the driveway of a three-story estate in Buckhead. The house sat far back from the street, up on a hill, and the SUV muscled its way up the windy driveway.

"Is that the van?" she questioned, looking over to where the glossy black Mercedes sprinter van sat over to the right of them in front of one of the three car garages.

"Yes, I believe that's the one," Pastor James replied, but he wasn't one-hundred percent sure.

A smile spread across her face so wide that she had covered her face with her hands to hide it.

"Can you drive that back to the church?" James asked her.

"I sure can," she responded.

James switched off the engine and removed his seat beat.

"Come with me," he said, opened his door and then stepped out. She got out of the passenger seat and closed the door behind her. They both walked around to the front of his SUV. She stood there with him and then he pulled out his phone and punched in his brother's number. "You home?" James said when Jamal answered.

"Yes, where you at?" he asked from the other end.

"Outside in your driveway and I need to get back to the church a.s.a.p. so open the door," James instructed.

"Come on in," Jamal returned and then ended the call.

James started towards the front door and Annabelle followed behind him until they made it up the steps and to the door.

Jamal opened the door and looked at his brother, then his

eyes went straight to Annabelle and he stared at her for a brief moment.

"Come on in," Jamal said, breaking his gaze.

James allowed Annabelle to walk in first and then he walked in behind her and shut the door. They stood in the foyer and then Jamal offered them a seat.

"It's not going to take me long to get dressed, so you two can have a seat," he said and moved quickly to the stairs.

James called out to him. "I thought you weren't going." His eyes followed him up the stairs.

"Why? When I told you I would," he answered and ran up the stairs. They sat and about thirty minutes later, a sharp dressed Jamal returned to the living room.

James looked at his watch and then at Jamal. "Finally," James said.

"Look, I dressed as fast as I could," Jamal defended.

"I bet, but you knew I was coming, so you should have been dressed."

"True, but the thing is, I was going to back out of going, but when you showed up with that gorgeous sister, I changed my mind."

"Annabelle?" he quizzed.

"Yes, Annabelle. Where is she by the way?"

"I showed her to the bathroom," James said and just then Annabelle walked back into the living room.

"Well, I know we won't make it back in time for my class," she said, looking at Pastor James.

"I know Annabelle and I'm sorry. My brother was supposed to be ready."

"It's all good. Let me go and get the keys and we can head out," Jamal said and disappeared into the hallway.

Now that Pastor James knew his brother's motivation for going to service, he quickly warned Annabelle.

"Listen, this is my brother and I love him to death, but he is a ladies' man, so do not, I repeat, don't let the smooth taste fool you. Be careful around him, Annabelle. I saw the way he looked at you and trust me, he is going to try and holler at you. Now, if you can help him to get his life right and show him the path to Christ that would be the only dealings I'd recommend for you two. I just want him to get right, before it's too late."

Annabelle smiled. "Well, that doesn't matter because I have no time for relationships. I'm focused on my walk with Christ, so he doesn't stand a chance romantically with me, but as a servant of God, I'll always show a person the path to our Savior."

Jamal walked back into the living room and then he tossed a set of keys towards his brother and James caught them. They were the keys to the sprinter van, and James handed them over to Annabelle. "You can go ahead and start it up and we'll be out in a minute."

Annabelle turned and walked out the door. Jamal took that moment to detour his brother of any thoughts of Annabelle. "Look, I know you love women and have this pretty boy aura and everything, but please don't mess with this young lady here. She's my Sunday school teacher and she's genuine and on a path of righteousness."

"Aw'ight, big brah," he said and headed out the door and then he stopped, turned around and reached inside his inside jacket pocket and pulled out the check that James had asked for. He handed it to him and said. "Now, let's go; we don't wanna be late."

When James got outside, he saw Jamal heading towards the Sprinter van where Annabelle was already waiting in the driver seat. When he got into the passenger seat, all he could do was shake his head and walk on towards his SUV. He knew he couldn't control his brother, but he prayed that Annabelle was strong enough to resist his charming ways.

§●

"Fasten your seatbelt," was the first thing Annabelle said to Jamal.

Jamal pulled out a pair of expensive Versace shades and slid them on his face, then he fastened his seat belt. "You must be about to take me for a long ride," he teased seductively.

Annabelle let out a light-hearted laugh. *This dude is funny,* she thought to herself. She glanced over at him and she had to admit he was handsome. Thinking back to a short while ago when she saw him in his tank top and shorts when he let them in, she noted his chest was chiseled and he had washboard abs imprinted on his tank. Jamal was clearly a ladies' man as Pastor James confirmed, but he was a pleasure to look at. Not in her league anyway, she put her focus on the road and tried to ignore the fabulous fragrance that filled the cab of the van.

"Have mercy," she mumbled under her breath.

"What was that?" he asked.

"Ahhh, nothing, I was ... it was nothing. Sometimes I just talk to God out loud," she fumbled.

"Oh, okay," he said and put his attention on his cellphone. There were a few moments of silence, and Annabelle tried to focus on her vows to God and not the fine work of art that was sitting in the passenger seat.

The ringing of his phone, gave her the jolt that she needed to stop gazing in his direction from the corner of her eyes.

"Hello," he answered, and he put his phone on speaker.

"Where are you?" a female voice asked.

"On the way to church, I'm trying to get my life together," he quipped. Annabelle wanted to laugh, but she kept quiet.

"Church?" the woman questioned.

He looked over at Annabelle. "Yes church," he confirmed.

Annabelle glanced over at him when he repeated himself.

"So, is this a bad time?" she asked.

"It is, I'll hit you up later," Jamal said and hit end.

She did a quick glance over at him again. "Girlfriend?" she

asked. She wondered why that just jumped from her lips. It wasn't her business.

"Associate," he replied.

"Oh," she said following closely behind Pastor James. With both hands on the steering wheel she began talking to God silently. 'Father God, I'm not actually sure what's going on here, but all I ask of you is to please keep me protected. This is some kind of fineness in my presences Lord God and I cannot be tempted. Lead me to the rock Father and keep me on a righteous path. Please, oh, God,' she prayed and told herself not to look in Jamal's direction.

"What are you thinking about?" Jamal asked, interrupting her pleas to the Father.

Annabelle kept her eyes locked on the back of Pastor James' SUV to keep from looking at his beautiful face. "I was just asking God to protect me."

"From what?" he asked her, his eyes were straight on her.

"Life, unrighteous and things that are not good for me," she confessed, followed by a slight deep breath. She felt as if her throat was getting dry, and she was desperately trying to hold her composer together.

"Oh, so that works? You pray and ask God to magically make you right when you wanna do wrong?" He slightly pulled his shades down from his eyes and peeped across the top of them at her.

She looked over at him, there was that smile again. She couldn't help it, he was charming, and that was why she needed prayer. "No, that's not exactly how it works. You can't think of God as a magician. God is not a game or a wishing well. You have to believe that He'll guide your mind and heart to do what's right," she answered. She could tell that Jamal wasn't a big religious or God's man, so she didn't want to leave him open to misunderstanding who God is.

"Oh, I get it, it's like they say ask and you shall receive."

"Yes, exactly," she responded back. "But, you have to believe it and have faith that it will come to past."

"Wow, that's deep, so if I asked God right now to make you mine and believe it, he will let it happen for me?" he asked her, his smile had faded away and by the tone of his voice he was dead serious.

She swallowed hard and then let out a breath. She didn't believe the words that he just let escape from his lips. "Well Jamal, can I call you Jamal?"

"Yes, you can call me whatever you like," he joked.

"Well, Jamal," she said and smiled a little because he wasn't an irritating type of charming, he was cool with his. "If you pray that prayer, you will get it if it's best for me," she said as a matter of fact.

"You? Why only you?" he questioned.

"Well, as of now, I think I'm the only one here that is a true believer and worshipper of the Lord our God. Now, if you were to give your life to him and seek righteousness too, your prayers will be answered based on what's best for the both of us."

He smiled and just nodded. The van fell silent for a little while and then he asked her, "What did my brother tell you about me?"

Annabelle got quiet for a second and wondered if she should tell him what Pastor James had actually said about him. She hated telling lies to people, but she definitely didn't want to throw her pastor under the bus, so she went with half of what the pastor said. "He said that he hopes and pray that I can help you give your life to Christ. That's really what he wants for you."

"I don't know about all of that right now, but I do know what will sound even better."

"I'm listening," she said.

"If you let me take you out to dinner this evening, after church."

"I'm sorry, Jamal, but I'll have to decline on that. Thanks

anyway for the offer," she said tenderly, keeping her eyes locked on the road.

"I'm sorry?" he said as if he misunderstood.

"I said no, I can't go to dinner with you."

"And why not?" he quizzed. The sound of his toned implied that he had never been turned down before or he didn't expect someone like her to turn him down, either way, she could tell he was shocked by her answer.

"I just can't, okay?"

He stared at her from behind his shades, with a smile on his lips. She could tell the wheels were turning in his head.

"No, you're not going to make this easy for me," he said.

"Jamal, it's not about that. I'm not going to play hard to get, if that's what you're thinking. I am on a path with God and I'm not interested in dating anyone right now. Don't take it personal. I just don't date."

"So, hi about a fun outing, like a day at the park or something with your kids? My brother told me about how the church needed this van to do more activities with the kids, so maybe I can tag along with you to the Georgia Aquarium? James already told me that that's one of the places you're thinking of taking the kids. If I go, then it won't be a date."

Annabelle glanced at him again to see if he were serious. He was still looking at her, his arms folded across his chest as if he was waiting for an answer. *The man was good. Damn good and clever,* she thought to herself. How could she resist him when he wanted to include himself with an event for her Sunday school students?

She didn't say anything. "Well?" he said interrupting the decision-making thoughts that were now bouncing around in her head.

"Well, I guess," she finally agreed. She'd let him join her and the kids, but she had no plans of having any one on one time with Mr. Smooth. She was going to have to double down on her prayers to stay straight around him for sure.

Rubbing his hands together, he said, "Cool, and we can go eat afterwards." Annabelle knew that wasn't going to happen, but she decided to keep her mouth shut, so he wouldn't spend the rest of the ride trying to change her mind.

5

*J*ust two hours later, Pastor James was standing before his flock with both hands resting on either side of the podium, in the pulpit. The church was full that morning, with all of one hundred, maybe one hundred and twenty members attending, and emotions were on high because the praise team had just finished leading them in praise and worship. Ready to deliver the Word of God, Pastor James' eyes went down to his Bible and then back up to the saints of God that had come to receive God's message that morning.

"Everybody will go through something in life that they will not like but think about this... When you were in school, how many of you hated test time?" he asked, and several hands went up in the air. There was small laughter and mumbling and someone said, "Amen Pastor."

"It was the word test that we hated, just the thought of a test use to have me uneasy. But see, its several tests in life that we're going to go through that's going to have you uneasy. Now, imagine when the Devil throws us something out there that's tempting, our Faith is being tested right there. The test," he said clearly enough to be sure that everyone understood where he was coming from.

Chants and cheers and praises came from the audience, some of the ladies stood up and clapped. Jamal was sitting on the front row looking at his brother preach, he was watching him carefully, then when he said bow your head he bowed his head and allowed the words of his prayer to sink in. Jamal had money, but he knew that he wasn't living right, but somewhere in the back of his mind he felt as if he wasn't ready. Giving up a carefree life to be a bible toting church boy was never an image he had for himself. After the prayer was done Pastor James called him up to the front to introduce him.

"God is good saints and God will always make a way, you have to believe," he said, and the members yelled 'Amen, hallelujah and praise Him'. "And today I have to recognize my brother, Jamal. He has been a blessing to this church in so many ways and I want to give thanks to our God for sending him to help our church in our times of need. Come on up, Jamal," he said.

Jamal stood up and adjusted his jacket and tie. He walked up to the front of the church and stood next to his brother. James said into the microphone.

"I just wanted to let everyone know that my brother here is the main reason that our church continues going strong. The new van out there in the parking lot was donated to us for our youth and our members that don't always have a way to get here." Then he reached inside his jacket pocket and removed the check that he received that morning. "And this here is a check for twenty thousand dollars that he made out to us. Not me, but us." All the members then stood and gave God some praise. Jamal allowed his eyes to scan the church and he found Annabelle smiling and looking directly at him.

He stared at her for a moment and leaned over into the microphone and said, "All I can say is God is good and whatever I can do to help, ya'll beautiful people just let me know," he said and looked at his brother and James embraced him with a strong hug and held him until tears began falling down his cheeks. "I love you, bro and thank you. This really helps us," he whispered.

"I love you, too, big bro," Jamal said.

❦

AFTER SERVICE WAS DONE, JAMAL HURRIED OUT TO CATCH Annabelle. When he spotted her, she was talking to an elderly woman and even though he didn't want to interrupt, he had to make sure he asked her not to leave before talking to him. He had to go back inside to make sure James knew he needed a ride back to his home, but he didn't want Annabelle to slip away.

He cleared his throat. "Excuse me, Annabelle, right?" he said, pretending he wasn't sure if that was her name.

"Yes, of course, Jamal," Annabelle said.

"And you are?" he asked, extending a hand to the woman she was conversing with.

"Sister Jenkins," the woman replied. She didn't look too happy that he interrupted their conversation.

"Well, Sister Jenkins, I'm Jamal, Pastor James' younger brother."

"I know who you are," Sister Jenkins snapped back.

"Yes, yes, yes, from the introduction earlier in service," he said.

"Yes!" she shot him and then turned to Annabelle. "Listen, we'll talk later, young lady. Have a blessed day," she said and then slowly turned and walked away.

"Wow, I'm really sorry for interrupting," he offered up.

"Are you really?" she questioned, now with her arms folded across her breast.

He chuckled. "To be honest, I'm not," he admitted.

"I figured that much."

"I just wanted to catch up with you before you left. I have to run inside to remind James that I need a lift or if you could get me home that would be great."

"What makes you think I have a car?"

"I don't know." He hunched his shoulders. "I mean, I'm sure you can take me with the van."

"Well, Deacon Harris is going to use the van to get some of our member's home."

"Well, I guess I'll run in and wait for my brother," he said with a smirk on his face. He knew Annabelle was trying to play a little hard to get, but he was up for the chase.

"Look, I'll give you a ride. I do have a car," she said.

"Cool," he said and slowly moved his head up and down.

"I have to go back in for my purse, can you give me a minute?"

"I'll give you whatever you need, beautiful."

She rolled her eyes and then walked away. He stood there by the steps and watched the parking lot of member's chatting and getting into their vehicles to head home, to brunch or whatever their next destination was.

"Well hello," a woman's voice penetrated Jamal's ears.

He looked to the right to see a thick chocolate sister. She looked young and the dress she was wearing didn't look church appropriate he thought.

"Hi there," he said. She was bad, indeed, but she looked immature, thirsty and like trouble. He was a player and hadn't settled down yet, but he was selective with the company he kept, and this little honey was about to get her feelings hurt.

"Jamal, right?" she asked and licked her red lips.

"Yes, that's right. Hi can I help you?" he asked.

"My name is Summer, and I wanted to say thanks for your generous donations to our church. I mean, that was a hefty donation," she said, batting her eyes.

Ten years ago, Jamal would have been interested, but this pretty young thing wasn't about to join his team. She had Sugar Daddy written all over her face and hashtag Zaddy all over her

Instagram post, so Jamal hurried up her conversation. "Yes, it was and what can I do for you?"

"Whatever you'd like, I'm game for it all," she purred.

He was about to deflate her bubble, but Annabelle approached.

"Afternoon Summer, your mom is waiting for you to help her with clean up," Annabelle said.

"Sister Annabelle, good afternoon. I was just thanking Mr. Jamal for the donations," she said like a young lady, not like the naughty chick that was down for whatever a couple of seconds ago.

"You're welcome," Jamal said again. The young chocolate beauty, smiled, nodded and hurried back inside.

"Are you ready?" Annabelle asked.

"Lead the way," he said and followed Annabelle to her ride. He shook his head at the old Accord that looked as if it had been through the storm.

"This you?" he asked.

"Yes," Annabelle said as a matter of fact. He chuckled and shook his head.

"You can always Uber or wait for Pastor James," she said.

"Nah, nah, nah, it's cool," he said and opened the door.

He had second thoughts about sitting in her front seat in his designer clothes, and then he said there wasn't anything that the dry cleaners couldn't take care of. Once inside, he put on his seatbelt and noted that although her car was old, it was clean and the mango scent from her car freshener was nice.

"So, are you going to accept my dinner invitation?"

She shook her head. "You don't give up do you?"

"Not easily," he admitted.

"Well, stop asking please. First off, you are not a man of God and that means we are unevenly yoked and things will never work, so I know to just stay in my lane."

"See, that's what's wrong with Christians today," he said.

"What do you mean?"

"You're already frowning on me, just because I'm not all saved and what does that mean anyway? Saved from what? You can still get hit by a car, fall down a flight of stairs, or lose a loved one or your own life."

"I'm not frowning on you and since you are not saved, you won't get what it means to be saved. It's not easy to explain, but if you want to learn about Christ, I can teach you .... And, and, and to be unevenly yoked means, we won't be spiritually compatible."

He nodded. He wasn't in tune with all of that Bible and God stuff, so he just answered with logic. "Okay, hi will you know if we are compatible at all if you don't get to know me? I mean if you'd spend a little time with me, I can learn more about your God and you can learn a little bit more about me." She let out a breath and shook her head from side to side. "Fight it all you want, but you know I'm right."

They stopped at a light and she glanced at him.

"You're not right and although what you said makes sense, I can't go out with you Jamal, so please stop asking."

He felt defeated, but only for a moment.

"Well, I guess the trip with the kids is the only way I'm going to see you?"

"Yes, if you're still interested."

"I am." He smiled. "Just let me know when and I'm there."

"I was thinking next Saturday afternoon."

"Cool, what's your number?"

She looked at him, and then proceeded because the light turned green.

"I'll let Pastor James know the date and time and he'll let you know."

He didn't push, because he knew he had to take it nice and slow with that one.

"That's cool," was all he said.

They rode the rest of the way to his place with chit chat about the service and the plans she had for the kids for the upcoming weeks. When she pulled in his driveway, he knew she'd decline coming in for a cocktail, but he asked anyway.

A couple of days later, he got a text from James telling him the time to meet up at the church for the trip. That Saturday evening, after Annabelle and Jamal had taken the kids to the Georgia Aquarium and to a pizza place to have an early dinner, he'd finally convinced her to let him take her out for a real grown up dinner.

🍃

HE TOOK HER TO RUTH'S CHRIS STEAK HOUSE IN ALPHARETTA Georgia. A cheerful young waiter escorted them to a nice secluded table for two, just behind them was a warm cozy fireplace and the ambiance was elegant. Jamal was just the perfect gentleman and Annabelle had to admit to herself that she was having a great time with him. He pulled her chair out for her and carefully pushed her up to the table, and then he sat across from her. The table was square and cover with a white linen table cloth and the table was set with beautiful china. Annabelle looked around at the restaurant.

"This is really nice, Jamal. Do you dine here often?" she asked.

"Yes, this is like one of my favorite restaurants in Atlanta," he said, and added, "And although most brag on the perfectly seasoned and mouthwatering steaks, the stuffed chicken here is like the best chicken in the world to me. And don't get me started on the sweet potato soufflé. It'll have you hooked."

"Look at you, all excited about food," she smiled. She admired his laidback demeanor. According to James, Jamal was a playboy, but he was charming, not arrogant and she found that attractive about him. He was persistent, and he always showed a sincere interest. A waiter approached their table a few moments later.

"Good evening, ma'am, sir," he greeted. "Can I get ya'll something to drank?"

"Water with lemons will be fine for me," Annabelle said.

"Water for me also, and a dirty goose martini," Jamal added. The server nodded and hurried away to fill their drink order. "Why you looking at me like that?"

She shrugged her shoulders and said, "No reason in particular." Annabelle smiled brightly at him to let him know that she liked his company. She was actually enjoying Jamal and she had a great time with him earlier that afternoon. He was great with the kids and demonstrated a level of patience that she hadn't expected.

He smiled back at her.

"You have a gorgeous smile you know that?" he complimented.

She blushed. "So, do you," she returned. Jamal was definitely easy on the eyes and she drew him in with her eyes.

"Thank you, Annabelle."

"I'm sure you get compliments all the time," she said.

"I do, but it is more refreshing when I get them from someone that I'm feeling."

"So, after one week, you know you're feeling me?" she questioned.

"Yes, and I'm so anxious to hear more about you. My brother speaks highly of you. I see that the kids love you and you seem to have your sh.., I mean stuff together."

"Well, there isn't much to tell. I moved to Atlanta a while ago and I'm just trying to adjust to my area and my new surroundings."

"I think there's more, but I won't push. I can tell you are a private person, Annabelle."

"Not really," she said, and just then, the server came with their drink orders. He asked if they were ready to order, but they hadn't even looked over the menu's yet, so the server said he'd come back in a few moments.

"As you were saying," he said and then sipped his martini.

"Well, like I said, it's not much to tell. What about you? I'm anxious to hear some things about you."

"Well, I'm thirty- eight years old," he started, but she cut him off.

"No, you're not, I refuse to believe that. Im'ma need see some ID please?" Annabelle joked and laughed lightly.

Jamal reached in his back pocket and pulled out his wallet and removed his driver's license and handed it to her. Curious, Annabelle took it and looked at it, she couldn't believe it.

"I would've thought you were at least twenty-nine or early thirties, but thirty-eight. I'm impressed. And you're a Gemini."

"You were only supposed to be looking at the year that I was born," he kidded.

His phone rung and he pulled it from his pocket. He looked at the screen and Annabelle watched him hurry to hit ignore. He placed his phone on the table and then went back to Annabelle as if the call hadn't come through.

"Now, back to what I was saying," he said and then sipped his drink. "Please don't believe everything you hear or read about Geminis. I'm far from crazy and there are not two-sides of me. I'm me, the same all the time," he stressed.

"Well, I have never experienced a male Gemini, so I won't judge." She smiled.

"Good," he said. The server came back over and still they were not ready.

"Listen, allow me to order for you," he offered.

"Okay, I trust you," She nodded.

"What do you like, steak or chicken?" he asked.

"Steak," she answered. He ordered, and the server took their menus and went to put their orders in. He sipped and was just about done but got back to the conversation.

"Well, other than the fact that I am a thirty-eight-year-old single Gemini, I run my own business on Shopify, and it generates great revenue. I have two car lots, one in Marietta and one in Dekalb, and I'm also a silent partner in an event planning company. We bring in concerts, comedy shows, festivals and plan parties. I don't have any kids and I love to travel."

Annabelle sipped her water from a straw and she listened to every word he said. Jamal was an interesting and even dateable, but she wasn't looking for a relationship or a boyfriend, so she hoped he didn't think that the dinner date meant that she was considering getting to know him romantically.

"Interesting. I see you have a lot going on with work and travels; maybe not a lot of time for a relationship or family?" she said, hinting that he was too busy to pursue her anyway.

"Well, people make time for the things they want to make time for." He smiled. He waved for the server to order another drink.

"Do you want a glass of wine? I mean I'm sure you don't drink, but a glass of red would compliment your meal," he offered.

She contemplated a moment and then said, "Sure. I mean I'd like that, but can you order for me, because I have no idea how to order wine."

"I got'chu," he said, and the server was there to get their drink order. His phone rang again, and Annabelle caught the words 'GOOD GOOD,' decorating his screen. He hit ignore again, but neither of them said anything about the call.

She sipped her water. "Well, compared to my boring and sad life, yours sounds amazing," she said and then her eyes were down towards the table.

"Really, enlighten me?" he inquired.

"Nah, a lot of stuff is too personal and trust if I share, you may not want to be associated with me anymore."

"Impossible." He smiled, but she shook her head. "Come on,

Annabelle; try me. I can't see you saying anything that horrible. I mean you're a church girl for crying out loud," he joked.

That made her feel a little more comfortable, but she was still a bit embarrassed and then she decided not to be ashamed. God had brought her through, and her circumstances were finally getting better, so she decided to be honest.

"Well, I'm a woman of God or a church girl as you put it, but I'm not perfect. I have a past, but I am striving for greatness. I don't have a prestigious job or own any property or fancy companies and my only job is at the church. I recently took the permanent position as Sunday school teacher because I needed the income. I haven't even gotten my first check," she sipped her water and then continued. "Up until a week ago, I was homeless, and I was staying at the women's shelter. I moved in with Sister Daisy from the church last weekend. I'm not sure if you know her, but she was the Sunday school teacher before me."

With a brow raised, he asked, "A shelter? Hi did that happen?" He folded his arms and leaned in a little.

"Life for me out in Augusta wasn't going so well. I had to deal with one situation after another and I just decided to leave. I came here to make a new start. I had some money saved up, so I got my car, with very little money left after that and it ran out fast. I was working for a while, living in hotels and renting rooms, but when I lost my last job, I ended up at the shelter."

"Damn Annabelle! You been going through it, baby," he said with concern and no judgment.

"Yes, but I've been pressing. I trust God, and I know God isn't going to put nothing on me that I can't handle."

"Well, I guess if you look at it from a religious view. I mean, I'm sorry to hear you've catching hell, babe," he said, and the server returned with their food and drinks. They shifted conversations during their meals. Annabelle even agreed to a second glass of wine. Once the table was clear and Annabelle declined on dessert, they went back to the previous conversation.

"You know, my brother always tells me that God blessed me to be in the position I'm in, but I just don't look at my life like that. I mean I do know that I'm fortunate and never take any of what I have for granted, but I don't always give God the credit for my hard work."

"Well, when you don't know God, your mindset is not of him, so that's why it has no connection with you, Jamal. But, if you pray and ask God to give you understanding and open the invitation for him to come into your life, you'd have a different prospective on things. Prayer is key. You don't have to be long and fancy, just speak to Him from your heart and I can guarantee you will start to slowly feel Him. Just start with a simple prayer in the mornings and just allow the Holy Spirit to enter into your life. It's like food for your soul. I can't explain it all right now, but I will help you, if you want to get to know Him."

Jamal listened attentively. She knew he was absorbing her words just by the way he looked into her eyes. "Will you pray with me every morning? I mean I will at least try. It would be nice to see what you and my brother sees."

"Yes, and you'd understand why I'm still standing and still pressing and still believing after all I've been through. You're questions of how do we do it will be answered. If you want me to call you every morning we can do it over the phone."

"Nah, that won't be necessary, because you will be waking up with me in the mornings. Then we can pray together." He clasped his fingers together and stared hard at her like he had the final word.

His tone was dead serious. Annabelle's head was already shaking side to side and she was wondering what her next response would be, because at that moment, she was at a loss for words. He was asking her to move in with him and she didn't know what to say. They had just met and she only shared one meal with him, so there was no way in hell was she just going to move in with him.

She stood. "Excuse me," she said and hurried off to the bathroom. When she got inside, she pulled out her phone and called Daisy Mae.

She answered on the third ring. "Hello," she answered pleasantly.

"Hey, Sister Daisy Mae?" Annabelle said nervously. She was trembling, and she wondered how Jamal had stirred up her insides like that in so little time.

"Yes, Annabelle. Are you okay, honey?"

"I, I, I'm fine. Why would you ask?"

"Because you don't sound fine."

Annabelle took a deep breath and tried to get her emotions under control. "I'm fine okay, no worries, but I have something I need to talk to you about tonight. Will you please wait up for me?"

"Of course, Annabelle. Are you sure you're okay?"

"Yes, I assure you. I will talk to when I get in."

"Okay," Daisy Mae said, and they ended the call.

Annabelle went into the stall to use the bathroom. Her mind was racing, and she wasn't sure what was happening. She was attracted to Jamal and found him to be interesting, but to just move in with him would be crazy she thought and said, "God please guide me and be my strength. Guide me in righteousness and your will may be done in my life," she prayed. She finished and washed her hands. She headed back to the table, so she could tell her date that his offer was absurd.

Yes, now she was feeling him and wanted to see him again, and even get to know him better. But, she knew better, so she'd had to let him know living with him wasn't an option.

When she got back to the table, Jamal wore a confident smile. She sat and then cringed because he looked so good sitting across from her. She didn't want to move in with him, but she did want to wrap her arms around his neck and do the tongue tangle with him. She had a vivid imagination as to rubbing her hands across his shoulders and down to the center of his back. *Come back, Anna.* She told herself. *Get a hold of yourself.*

"Are you alright, Belle?" he asked.

"Belle?"

"Yes, I think it fits you. Do you mind?"

Annabelle hunched her shoulders. She didn't mind if he called her that.

"Yes, I'm alright, and yes, you can call me, Belle. My family used to call me that when I was a kid."

"Listen at me real quick, I know what I said about waking up together every morning with me was a bit much, but I'm going to be honest, I'm really feeling you. You're the kind of woman I need in my life, Belle, and I don't need a ton of dates, text and phone calls to know that. I've wanted someone like you in my life for a very long time, so just think about it. I want a chance to show you that I'm for real about you. Just give me a chance," he said. He was serious, and Annabelle still sat there blinking, wondering how he knew for sure that it was her. Annabelle needed to think, and more importantly she needed to pray.

"I need you to take me home now, Jamal," she said while looking him in his eyes.

He nodded. "Okay," he agreed without rebuttal. He waved for the check and after he paid, he did what she asked and took her back to Daisy Mae's house.

6

*W*hen Annabelle got home, Daisy Mae was sitting in the living room waiting for her. She closed and locked the door behind her, and then she went and flopped down on the couch next to Daisy Mae and threw her head back. She took a deep breath and looked at Daisy Mae.

"A lot of stuff happened today."

"A lot of stuff like what?" Daisy Mae inquired.

"Well, for starters, I met Pastor James' younger brother, Jamal, last Sunday when we picked up the van from his house." She paused and took a deep breath and then went on, "He's nice and all, but he wants a relationship and he is certain that he wants to be with me, but I'm not sure if I'm ready to be in a relationship right now or if even I need to be thinking of a relationship."

Daisy Mae patted Annabelle on her thigh.

"Why not? You're young and there are no reasons for you to not give it a try."

Annabelle sighed. "I just want my life to be right with God."

"Okay, and no man can stop that unless you allow him. Is he against you going to church or does he have a problem with religion?"

"No, but he's not saved."

"Well, maybe you can be the person to lead him to Christ. A relationship isn't marriage, Annabelle. Do you like him?"

She smiled brightly. "Yes, that is the problem Daisy Mae. I mean I more than like him. And it's strange how I feel so strongly about him when it's been less than a week since meeting him."

"Well, I know about love at first sight. It happens you know."

"Well, I never knew that until now. I mean, when I'm around him I just feel like I'm going to come undone. The way he looks at me, Daisy Mae, makes me feel special. Even after I told him about my situation, he still looked at me the same as before he knew."

"Well, that sounds like a good thing, Annabelle."

"Yes, but I'm not sure if Jamal wants the same things out of life that I want."

Daisy Mae sat quiet for a moment and then she turned her body to face Annabelle and then reached for her hands. "As women, baby, sometimes we just have to follow our hearts. Only time will tell if Jamal will desire the things you do, but you have to give it a chance to find out. I'm not saying not to be cautious, just don't rule anything out."

"I understand that, I just don't want to put myself in a position that I will regret later on," Annabelle said.

"Always remember this, God always protects his children, regardless of the situation. You just continue to pray about it and stay focused on your future. And who knows, God may be putting you in his life for a reason also."

Annabelle smiled. "I've thought about that part also. I mean, he really seems like a decent man but..."

"There are no buts, baby," Daisy Mae said. "It's a blessing waiting for you so great that you'll be blown away when you get it. Just watch." She leaned over and kissed Annabelle on her cheek. "Now, go get you some rest because you got a big day tomorrow." She stood up and walked towards her room,

Annabelle looked after her until she disappeared from her sight. Then, she stood up herself and headed to her bedroom. She undressed and went into the bathroom to shower. When she came back out, she followed her same routine and got on her knees on the side of the bed and started praying.

"Dear father, I'm not sure what the next step for me is or what you got planned for my future, but I'm not going to question you. I do hope and pray that you'll protect me physically, spiritually and mentally. I would like to send a special prayer up for Jamal, Sister Daisy and my old friend from the shelter, Angel. In Jesus name I pray, Amen." She stood up and turned the room light out and climbed into bed.

The following morning, Annabelle got up and it was cold and raining outside. She was standing in front of the window in the living room looking out through a small slit in the curtain. The rain was coming down hard and she stared at a mud puddle in the front yard, lost in her thoughts about Jamal. She didn't like that the thought of him having her whole entire body tingling and she had to admit that she wanted him. Her cell phone rung and she went to the sofa and picked it up. The number on the screen wasn't familiar to her, but she slid the green button to the side and answered.

"Hello."

"Good morning, Belle," Jamal said.

Hearing his voice melted her heart. Smiling, she said, "Good morning to you, Jamal." She walked back over to the window and looked out for a minute.

"I prayed this morning when I got up, well I'm not actually out the bed yet but I wanted to let you know that." His voice was smooth, deep and relaxing.

"Did it make you feel better?" she asked.

"Of course, it did. That's why I wanted to call you. I was up most of the night thinking of you and I wanted to know if I could see you today, maybe breakfast or something."

Annabelle closed her eyes, her lips pressed together, and she just shook her head side to side before she answered.

"Yes, where do you want to meet?"

"Nowhere, I'm coming to get you. Give me about an hour, okay?"

"Okay," she chirped happily and hung up the phone. Then, she took a deep breath and turned around and saw Daisy Mae standing there with a smile on her face.

"Baby, when I tell you that you are glowing this morning, you know how ya'll young girls be saying the 'Glow up is real'. Your happiness is what matters most," Daisy Mae said.

Annabelle walked over to her and hugged her.

"I know and thank you. I am happy for a change." They stood there for a minute and rocked side to side while Daisy Mae rubbed her hand up and down her back.

"It's time for you to enjoy yourself a little," Daisy Mae added, and Annabelle agreed.

When Jamal pulled up into Daisy Mae's driveway it was still pouring. Annabelle was peeping through the curtains and saw him pull up. He was in a different car, a black Porsche Panamera and Annabelle's eyes widened. The headlights were still on and when the driver side door opened. The first thing that she saw was a big plaid Burberry umbrella pop up and then he stepped out. She watched him make his way to the front porch and then she closed the curtains. Annabelle went to the door to let him in. She opened the door and he was standing there shaking the water from the umbrella.

"Hello." She smiled.

"Hello." He smiled back at her.

"Do you wanna come inside?" she asked.

"I shouldn't because my shoes are still wet. Are you ready to go?" His voice was smooth, deep and charming all in one.

She nodded yes and then grabbed her purse from the coat rack that stood close by the door. She stepped out onto the front

porch, and he quickly leaned down and gave her a quick hug and
a kiss on her cheek.

"You lookin' spectacular," he complimented.

"Thank you." Her eyes looked him up and down, and then
she said, "You are, too."

"Thank you, now just imagine how good we're going to look
together," he said, but Annabelle didn't comment. She closed the
door to the house and locked it with her key. Before they stepped
down the porch, Jamal opened the umbrella and placed it over
Annabelle's head. They walked to the car, but instead of walking
her to the passenger side, he took her around to the driver's side.
"I want you to drive. I don't like driving in the rain."

She looked up at him. "I don't mind driving," she said. Jamal
opened the door for her and she got in. The car was still running.
He closed the door behind her and walked around to the
passenger side, and got in.

He closed his umbrella and put it in the backseat. Then he
looked at her.

"Damn! You look good behind the wheel, Belle. Go wherever
you want to, I'm riding with you today."

Annabelle put on her seatbelt and put the car in reverse.
Before long the hard rain had settled to a light drizzle. She
glanced over at him and then looked back at the street.

"What about your place?" she suggested and looked at him.
His mouth opened, and nothing came out. She knew that
shocked him.

"Ummm, yeah sounds like a plan to me," he said with a
devilish grin on his face. Annabelle's stomach got butterflies, but
she decided to relax and go with the flow. She felt comfortable
with Jamal, so she pressed the gas and gave the Porsche some
power. Since the ground was still wet from the rain, she kept both
hands on the wheel, and she breezed through traffic like the she
was the owner of that car. She was stopped at a light, so she
looked over at him. He was doing something with his phone, so

she cranked up the volume on the radio. Anita Baker's *Rapture of Love* was coming through the speakers and she felt that that was the perfect song to cruise to that rainy afternoon. The light changed, and she proceeded bobbing her head to the music.

"You like that song?" Jamal asked.

She smiled. "I do."

He bobbed his head along with her and then he started singing the song to her. Annabelle looked at him blushing. "Nothing else can compare," he sang along with Anita and reached over for her hand.

Then Annabelle started singing the song also, word for word.

"You too young to know about that Anita baker," he teased playfully.

"You're right, but that was my mother's favorite song," That song brought back fond memories of her momma, and she smiled thinking of her. Funny, how of all the songs in the world, they'd play that one. She missed her momma and a tear rolled down her face.

Jamal reached over and wiped the tear from her face.

"You don't have to cry no more, baby. I got you now and everything is going to be fine."

Annabelle turned her attention back to the road and tried not to let her emotions damper her day. Jamal's phone rung and his brother James' name came across the screen. He quickly ignored the call and they rode the rest of the way letting the radio play. By the time they arrived at Jamal's house the rain had completely stopped. Jamal pressed the remote above Annabelle's head on the visor and the middle door of the three-car garage rose up.

"Pull in," he told her.

Annabelle pulled the Porsche into the garage, and to her right there was a yellow Ferrari parked. Annabelle put the Porsche in park and killed the engine.

"Tell me you know how to cook," he said while opening the door and getting out.

Annabelle got out and looked at Jamal over the top of the car.

"I'm a pretty good cook," she said, and they walked inside the house through the side door. Jamal's home was beautiful, she noticed, as he gave her a tour. They ended the tour in his kitchen. The floor was covered with Apricot colored marble, there were top of the line appliances, with granite tops and a stove in the center island. Annabelle looked up, the ceiling was nearly twenty feet high. That was a woman's dream kitchen and if she had to cook in there, she'd be fine with that. Jamal pointed to the stainless-steel refrigerator.

"Everything that you need is in there."

"What do you want to eat?" she asked him.

Jamal walked up close to her, his lips nearly touching hers, and then he whispered, "You." And then he kissed her softly. She kissed him back, allowing his lips to play around on hers. Annabelle closed her eyes and wrapped her arms around his neck. Jamal placed his hands at the small of her waist and pulled her close to his body. Annabelle was on fire and only he could cool her down. She moved her hands underneath his shirt and caressed his muscular chest. Jamal picked her up as if she didn't weigh a pound and carried her up the stairs and into his bedroom. Inside the bedroom, Jamal sat her down on the bed and pulled his shirt up over his head. She laid there looking up at him. His body was hard as a rock, and his muscles were chiseled from his waist up to his neck.

"Are you sure this is what you want?" he asked her.

Annabelle looked nervous, but she nodded her head.

Jamal stood there in front of her and started unfastening his pants. When he pulled the zipper down and pulled his pants down, she couldn't believe the huge bulge in his white and gold colored Versace briefs. Annabelle sat up, her face was at his waist line. She reached and touched him. Massaging him with her hands. She looked up at him and whispered, "I can't believe this."

Her heart was beating faster now, and she was still rubbing and stroking him.

"I'm not sure if I can take it. I never had sex before."

Jamal twisted his mouth in one corner. "Stop playing."

"I'm serious, I'm a virgin," she confessed, looking him in the eyes. He reached down and smoothed her hair down. Jamal sat down on the bed next to her and they laid back together, he carefully pulled her into his arms.

"I'm not going to rush you into nothing that you don't want to do."

Annabelle was resting her head on his chest, she felt so comfortable with him, she could hear him breathing and feel his chest rising and falling in a smooth movement. In her mind she wanted to have sex, but her heart was telling her something totally different. Then she asked him, "If we start and it starts to hurt too much will you stop?"

"Of course, I'll stop, but really I think we should hold off, Belle. I mean as bad as I want you, I've never met a grown ass woman that was still a virgin."

Annabelle rolled over and got out the bed.

"I'm going to the bathroom," she said, then she turned around and walked away not responding to his last statement. She closed the door behind her.

By the time Annabelle came back from the bathroom he was sleeping good. Annabelle walked out in her bra and panties and she was carrying her clothes in her hand. She placed them in a chair that was sitting in the corner. Then she walked over to the bed where Jamal was sleeping, she climbed up next to him and when she touched his body he woke up and looked at her.

"Are you tired?" she asked him while allowing her hand to move easy down his cheekbone.

Jamal smiled. "Was I asleep?"

"Yes, you were snoring like a bear," she said.

"I'm sure. When I was younger I was told that I have a

sleeping disorder called Narcolepsy, but I'd refused to believe it because I've never fell asleep in public or while talking to people. Only when I laid down. Immediately my body shuts down," he said and pulled her body closer to his. Jamal removed her bra strap down her shoulders and he cupped them both at the same time. Annabelle liked that, his hands were strong, and his touch was making her hot. She closed her eyes and her breathing was getting heavy, she took his right hand and moved it down between her legs. Annabelle was already moaning and squirming around.

"Oh. God," she said and wondered if she should turn back. Her flesh took the lead and she moaned as he rubbed her center.

"Relax, baby," he coached. I want you to enjoy it. Now lay back and relax," he said and climbed on top of Annabelle. He was on his knees between her legs holding his hard, thick member and slowly moving the head up against her wet vagina. She tried to brace herself to receive him, but when Jamal finally pushed the head of his penis inside of her, she let out a scream and placed her tiny hands in the center of his chest.

"I'm not going to hurt you. Just let me know when to stop."

Her eyes showed fear and pain all at the same time as she nodded her head up and down. Jamal pushed more of himself inside of her and her walls were so tight it felt like he was ripping her apart. He looked at her, her eyes were closed, and her mouth was gaped open.

"How it feel?"

"It hurts, and it burns, but I'm okay," she whispered. She turned her head to the side and tried to endure and prayed that it would get better soon.

"You want me to stop?"

"No," she moaned. "Just go slower."

Jamal slowed down, but her face said it all. She wasn't enjoying it.

"You ready for me to stop?" he asked her.

As much as she wanted to keep going, she finally gave up. "Oh, God! Yes, please stop."

Jamal stopped moving but he didn't pull out of her. "Just relax, it will get better."

She shook her head.

"Okay, let's just stop for a little while then."

"Yes, please, for a little while."

He pulled himself out of her and rolled over on his back and laid next to her. Annabelle didn't move, she just laid there with her legs open, her vagina was aching, wishing she had held on to her virginity. She really cared for Jamal, but she didn't love him.

She didn't want to move.

Jamal touched her, and she jumped. He pulled his hand back.

"Belle, baby, are you okay?" he asked her tenderly.

"Just throbbing and aching. I didn't know that it would be this bad," she said.

"Well, the first time is always the worse and I'm going to go and fill this Jacuzzi tub up for you with some hot water and bath oil. After a soak and some relaxation, you will feel better." She nodded with a little smile.

"It won't be the bad the next time," he said.

"Are you sure?"

"Not one hundred percent, but I know it won't be as awful as I loosen you up. Now, come on and soak and I'll go down and whip us up something to eat." He rolled out of the bed and then grabbed some sweats. He walked into the master bathroom and started the water and then went into his linen cabinet and grabbed a new sponge. He tossed it into the tub and then Annabelle walked in with her arm across her breast and her other hand in front of her center. She knew he had already seen her naked, but it was odd walking around naked.

"It will take the water a little time to fill. Come here and let me help you get in," he said with an outstretched arm. She took it and he held her hand as she stepped in the tub. Once she was in, she laid back.

"Once the water rises above the jets, just press this button," he instructed, and she nodded. He added some fragranced oil and then he went underneath his cabinet and grabbed the Epsom Salt and sprinkled a bit into her bath. "This will help soothe the throbbing."

She nodded again. "Thank you, Jamal. I'm sure this will definitely help."

"Now, I'm going down to make something to eat."

"Okay," she said. Once he was gone, she took a look around his huge master bath. It had double sinks with the same granite that was in his kitchen. The marbled floors were the same, and the entire walls underneath the lighting were mirrored. Once the water rose higher, she turned on the jets and laid back to relax.

Within minutes, the aroma of food was in the air and Annabelle couldn't wait to put a meal in her stomach. After almost thirty minutes of soaking and relaxing, she grabbed the sponge that was that was floating around the tub and washed her skin. She got out and dried off with the folded towel that was on the vanity and then wrapped it around her body.

She went into his master bedroom and took a seat on the plush chair and he walked in.

"Are you alright, baby? Did the soak help?" he asked.

"Yes. Still a tad bit sore, but I'm okay." She smiled and then stood. She walked over to him and wrapped her arms around his neck and he pulled her into his hard body.

"Damn! You definitely don't have a problem getting wet." He smiled. "Look at the sheet," he said, and she turned to see what he was looking at.

"Is that not normal? I mean since this was my first time, I don't know what my body supposed to do or not do."

"Nah, baby, that there is normal as hell!"

"Jamal, language. I don't like that kinda of talk."

"My bad babe, but that is normal and sexy," he said and planted a couple of kisses on her lips.

She blushed. "Maybe the next time I'll be able to please you better."

"Listen, don't worry, baby. I will teach you and before you know it, you'll be loving it, too."

"So, you will be patient with me," she asked nervously.

"No doubt, baby. And I'm going to teach you so many things and we are going to experience so many pleasing things together, just wait and see," he said, giving her that same devilish grin he gave her earlier.

"Awwww you got it like that," she said.

"Yes, nd let me give you something to slip on so you can come down and eat. I made steaks, baked potatoes and steamed vegetables."

"All for me, I'm impressed."

"Baby, you ain't seen nothing yet," he said and then went for his drawer. He gave her an oversized Tee and after she put it on they headed downstairs.

"How about some music, do you like ole school?"

"Yes." She smiled, and he grabbed a remote and the sounds of Cheryl Lynn's *Encore* oozed from the speakers. "Yes, that cut right there is nice," Annabelle said, moving a little to the beat.

"Indeed, that is a jam," he said, taking plates from the cabinets. "Have a seat, baby," he said.

"You don't need any help?"

"Nah, I got this and as I said before, I got you."

"I hear you, Jamal, but I don't want to move too fast," Annabelle said.

"What's the definition of fast? I mean if you feeling me like I'm feeling you let's just dive right in and do this. Time is precious, and we know we want each other, Belle, so stop with this hesitation. I want you and I want you to be my woman." She looked at him with a look of suspicion. "Don't look at me that way, Belle. I know James said I was a player and truthfully, I was, but it is something different about you and my appetite for you is strong, so trust me and let me show you a new world. I won't hurt you, baby, just believe in me and let me have you."

She held on to his words and they were like music to her ears. She wanted to be loved, taken care of and to be treated to nice things. Would it be so bad to dive right in? *God help me*, she silently prayed.

"Can we just have dinner for now and just spend a little more time together? I mean, I'm really feeling you, too, baby, but I have to be careful with the choices I make."

He put her plate in front of her. "I hear you, Belle, but you have to live a little. I know you and God tight and all that jazz, but I know God wants to see you happy and wants you to enjoy your life. My brother, James, tells me that mess all the time. James is a pastor and a man of God, but he isn't uptight, so please just allow me to show you that I'm for real," he said.

Annabelle smiled and exhaled and said, "Okay, Jamal, I want whatever you want."

"That's my girl," he said and after he gave her a wet kiss. He sat across from her and they enjoyed their dinner with nonstop conversation.

7

By the time night fell, Annabelle was still with Jamal at his house. Although she wasn't ready to leave, it was getting late and she needed to head home. When she told him that it was time for her to head back to Daisy Mae's house he asked, "What time are you coming back?"

"What do you mean, Jamal?" she asked.

"I mean, I want you to come back and stay with me," he said and pulled her into his arms again, where she had been most of that day. "I wanna wake up with you in my arms in the morning. I'm for real about us praying together. If we pray together we'll stay together," he said, laying on the charm.

"I'll have to think about that, Jamal. I mean, today was beautiful and I don't wanna leave you, but spending the night is a bit much and living together Jamal is a huge deal."

"Well, I tell you what then, I own a one-bedroom in midtown. It's fully furnished and vacant. I want to help you, Belle, and set you up right. I don't want my woman sleeping in someone's spare room. You believe in God and know he is going to provide for you, right? So, don't block your blessing. I'm in a position to help you so let me do that. God is putting all of this on my heart for you, so just let me help you."

Annabelle stood there for a moment and he could tell she was contemplating his offer, but when she spoke he knew she wasn't going to be an easy win.

"I don't know, Jamal. Just please get me back to Daisy Mae's house and let me think on it."

He shook his head. "You got a Porsche out there in the garage, so if you want to head back to Daisy Mae's you can drive yourself."

"Come again?"

"You heard me, Belle. The car is yours for as long as you want. Just go home and grab your things and come back here, or as I offered the rental unit. Either way, I got you."

"How do I explain a Porsche, Jamal? I am a Sunday school teacher and Pastor James is going to know I got it from you. I don't want him to know that we've been intimate." She began to tremble.

"Let me worry about Pastor James, okay? Once I show him that my intentions with you are genuine, and not of evil, he'll come around."

"Yeah but...," she disputed, but his kiss cut off her words.

Looking her in her eyes, he said, "You must trust me on this one. I got the entire church with me, and if they with me, they with you. They know I'm no bible totting church boy, but they love and respect me. Now, go and get your clothes and come back to me tonight."

Annabelle nodded, and he knew she believed his words. She went up on her tippy toes and kissed him. "I'm going to trust you on this, Jamal, but don't think I'm crazy when you hear me talking to God out loud every day."

"I already know I'm giving my heart to a church girl so don't worry," he said.

"Okay, I'm going to get my things and I'm sure Daisy Mae

won't mind my car being there for a few days, until we can pick it up."

"Baby, you can give that car to Daisy Mae, donate it to one of your church friends, because my woman is too classy to not roll in luxury."

She smiled again. "Maybe you were sent from heaven."

"You ain't seen the half. Now, go and hurry back." With that Annabelle dressed and made her exit.

Once the garage door closed, Jamal went upstairs and took a shower and brushed his teeth. He then went to his dresser, opened the top drawer, dug into the corner and pulled out a pill bottle. He twisted the top, removed the lid and dumped a Xanax bar in his hand. He sat it on his tongue and went into the bathroom and swallowed it down with some cold water from the sink. He went back downstairs, sat on the couch and called his brother. He hit the speaker button and James' voice came through after the second ring. "Hello," he said.

"What up, big brah? How everything going with you?"

"Nothing, too much, Jamal," he said. "What's going on?"

"I fucked up, man."

"How? What happened?"

"Annabelle happened."

"But Jamal, what did I tell you about pursuing that woman. Are we hiding things from each other now?" James barked into the phone.

"Nah brah, no secrets or games this time, and I'm telling you what's good this time."

"You the reason why we can't keep the good women at the church now, you can't have sex with every new face that joins the church, Jamal. I asked you to stay away from Annabelle. She is a good girl on a righteous path."

"I know, brah, and you are right. I'm trying to get my life together too and I need a woman like her to help me change. Annabelle can help me, I know it."

"We'll see in the near future if that statement is true or false."

Jamal looked at the phone, he knew he'd let his brother down a few times in the past when he was dealing with the church members. Things really took a turn when he messed around with this one particular chick at the church that was an ex stripper. She'd turned her life around, but she was too beautiful to pass up. Her body was sculpted into perfection and the first time Jamal laid eyes on her, he had to have her. She had a boyfriend who was an ex-navy seal, but that didn't stop Jamal. After a while of messing around, her man grew suspicious and decided to follow her one day. She led him to Jamal's house and he made a big scene at the house. The neighbors called the police and Jamal thought things were done after the police took him away, but the boyfriend didn't stop there. He showed up at the church one Sunday and made another scene by standing up in the front of the church revealing Jamal's affair with his girlfriend.

"I'm looking for the pretty nigga that's been creepin' with my fiancée," he blasted, and the entire church went into an uproar. It was a good thing that Jamal wasn't there that day because it probably would have been far worse; Jamal thought about all this and said to his brother.

"I'm going to do right by this one or die trying."

"Watch what you speak into the atmosphere, Jamal," he said and then ended the call. Jamal laughed at him when he hung up.

"Damn! He must be big mad about me taking Annabelle."

He tossed his phone on the couch next to him and just shook his head. Jamal kicked his feet up on the sofa and fell asleep. It was after eleven when Annabelle woke him. He looked at her two suitcases near the door and asked, "How long you been here?"

"I just walked in."

"I'm glad you came back. You had me a little worried."

"There is no need to worry, it's in God's hands now, and when his hands are in it, it's out of our control." She kissed him on his cheek and said, "Are you gonna help me get the rest of the clothes out of the car?"

Jamal sat up and stretched. The Xanax pill that he'd taken earlier had had him feeling sluggish.

"Yeah babe, I'll get everything else," he said and headed toward the garage to unload her things.

§▲

WHEN SUNDAY ROLLED AROUND, ANNABELLE AND JAMAL RODE TO church together in her Porsche. Jamal reclined in the passenger seat and hummed to the gospel tunes that Annabelle insisted that they listened to. They were both casually dressed, but Jamal was decked out in his Gucci dress shoes, gray pants and a Gucci blazer. Although Annabelle had a new wardrobe of clothes she still wasn't flashy, so her outfit didn't standout. They pulled into the parking lot and parked in a reserved space. Church didn't start until ten, but Annabelle had a Sunday school class to teach at nine. Jamal saw his brother's SUV in the parking lot, so he knew that he was already inside.

They got out the car and walked inside the church and headed toward the back where Pastor James' office was at. Jamal looked at Annabelle and said, "Go ahead and handle your business with the kids and everything and I'll go in here and talk with my brother." He gave her a quick kiss and she smiled and walked away.

She headed towards the classroom to put her things down and was surprised to see the room empty. She put her bag, Bible and purse down and then headed to the sanctuary. She opened the doors and to her surprise, Sister Daisy Mae was with the kids having prayer. She didn't want to interrupt Sister Daisy Mae, so she went over to join them. They were all holding hands in one big group circle for prayer. She stopped just behind them and bowed her head.

"And Lord Jesus, these children are our future, keep them protected, raise them up with righteousness and your holy spirit. Bless each and every last one of them with good health, and remove them from poverty Lord God," Daisy Mae prayed. She paused and cleared her throat and then continued, "We love you Lord Jesus and we thank you this day for life. We know without you we wouldn't exist and all things we ask, we ask in your son Jesus' name. Amen."

When Annabelle opened her eyes, there was a circle of kids smiling at her. "Miss Annabelle," a young girl said and rushed over to hugged her. She was eleven years old and her name was Treasure. Annabelle hugged her back and rubbed her head.

"Good morning, Treasure," she said and looked around at everyone else and said, "Good morning."

They all said, "Good morning," in unison. Daisy Mae walked over to Annabelle and hugged her with a warm embrace. "Good morning," Daisy Mae said.

"Good morning, Sister Daisy Mae," Annabelle responded.

"I'm glad you made it, baby," Daisy Mae said and released her embrace. She looked at the kids and said, "Ya'll can go into the classroom." The kids did as they were told, and Daisy Mae turned her attention back to Annabelle.

"So, how are you?" Daisy Mae asked, her eyes fixed directly on her.

"I'm fine, Sister Daisy. I didn't expect to see you this bright and early, since I'll be teaching the class."

"Well, I'm feeling better and I am accustomed to getting here on Sundays at this time. I know I'm old and Pastor and the deacons want to give you the job, but I'll still be here early and sit in with the class, too. Those kids are my heart and I can agree to step down as the teacher, but I'm not going to miss the class," she said from the heart and with an overwhelming smile.

"So, you are okay with me filling the role permanently?"

"Yes, I'm okay with that."

"I was a bit hesitant to take the offer."

"I'm sure you were, that's why you didn't tell me." She smiled.

"I was just waiting for the right time. I honestly still had reservations about it."

"Well, no worries. God isn't a God of confusion or disorder. When Pastor James told me that he thought it would be best since I am getting up in age, I agreed with him, so we are good Annabelle. We are sisters in Christ and you are like a daughter to me, so don't ever be afraid to tell me something."

Annabelle nodded. "Yes, ma'am."

"Now, we should head to class, before we fall too far behind," Daisy Mae said, going for her purse, and Bible that sat on the front pew. Before they could make their exit, Jamal and Pastor James walked into the sanctuary.

"Morning Sister Daisy, Annabelle," Pastor James said.

"Morning Pastor," Daisy Mae said and then Annabelle.

"Good to see you, Sister Daisy Mae," Jamal said and went in to hug her.

"Good to see you, too, Jamal."

"Listen Annabelle, I wanted to speak to you really quick, if you have a moment," Pastor James said.

"Sure, Pastor James."

"Daisy Mae, could you give us a moment?"

"Yes, I'll go in and get the kids started for you, Annabelle. What's todays lesson going to be about?"

"Exodus twenty verse twelve. I want to teach them about how important it is to honor their parents."

"Good topic and you," Daisy Mae said pointing a finger at Jamal. "I know you have a past young man, this entire town knows it, but I don't judge, and I see you've changed over the years. Annabelle is more than a friend, she is like a daughter to me, so you better do right by her, you hear?" Daisy Mae said.

"Yes ma'am. You have my word. The things I used to do, that

ain't me no more, Sister Daisy, and I give you my word that I will take care of Annabelle."

She hugged him. "Aw'right, Jamal. I will be praying for you both," she said.

Jamal nodded. "Yes ma'am," he said.

Annabelle smiled, and Daisy Mae made her exist. Both Jamal and Annabelle's eyes landed on Pastor James.

"So, after talking to my brother, I know that you two have decided to have a relationship. Now, I'm not your dad, I'm your pastor and all I ask is to keep your relationship at home and not here. I didn't agree with you and Jamal getting together, but you two are adults and can do what you choose. I will pray for you two and ask God to guide your steps. And if you two make it to exchange vows, I'll be honored to officiate the ceremony."

"Thank you, Pastor," Annabelle said, giving him a hug. Her heart was smiling just as well as her face, this was defiantly something that she needed to hear because it was really worrying her.

"Yes, James I appreciate you, bro, and I know you have your concerns, but my past is my past and I'm not that man anymore. My intentions are all good for Annabelle, you'll see."

"On that note, let me head back to my office to get prepared for this morning's service and you, Annabelle, get to your class," Pastor James said with a jokingly smile.

"Yes sir," she said. James walked away first and Annabelle turned to Jamal.

"Both Daisy Mae and Pastor mentioned your past. Should I be concerned?" she asked him with a questioned look.

"No, baby, it's just that I dated a member before and it just didn't go too well. She lied and didn't tell me she was involved with someone and things got a little ugly, but that was years ago and trust, that is all behind me," he said as he was taking her by her hands.

She smiled. "Okay, babe. Let me get to my kids." She moved in closer to him and they hugged for a brief moment, Jamal rubbed her back for a moment and he held onto her with a tight squeeze.

"Yes, and I'm going to head up the street and grab some coffee." He kissed her on her cheek.

"Okay," she said, and they parted ways.

Later that afternoon after church, Jamal prepared for a trip he had to take to Colorado. The trip had been planned prior to meeting Annabelle and even though it was last minute, and the ticket would be beyond expensive, he invited her to go with him. She declined, and he did not like her answer.

"Why not, baby?" he asked her. His tone of voice was low and nearly sad.

"Because it's so last minute. I have barely unpacked and settled in. I can get some things done while you're away."

Jamal was quiet for a moment and then he took a long deep breath and said, "We're coming back tomorrow night though, Belle; the trip is only for a day."

Annabelle placed her hands on her waist and looked up at him, then she smiled. "Well, I guess I can go. One day isn't long," she said, and he pulled her into his arms.

"Good. It's cold out there, so let's slide by Lenox mall real quick and we can head straight to the airport from there."

"Okay," she agreed. They packed a couple of essentials and then headed to the mall. When they were leaving the mall, Jamal was on his iPhone in a heated discussion with someone.

"I don't care, that's not what we agreed upon, Andrew," he blasted into the phone with a screwed-up face. He paused and, then he looked over at Annabelle. "You know how to get to the airport from here?"

She nodded her head and said, "Yes."

"But what did you tell me?" he said into the phone again.

Jamal listened for a moment and then he said, "Dude, you must be losing your mind, because that's not what you said. You told me to get you two hundred thousand and give you forty-five days; you said you had the building is that not what you told me, Andrew?"

Jamal got quiet again and while he listened, he just nodded his head. Then he said into the phone. "I'm very aware of the marijuana dispensaries revenue in Colorado, that's why I want in. But, if you can't handle the paperwork and business, I'll have to find someone else to handle that business for me!"

Jamal listened to whatever the guy on the other end was saying. He looked over at Annabelle and wished he could have had that conversation without her being present, but it was too late, he had already put his business out there. Back to his call, he said, "You know what Andrew, this is some bull and there is no point of me coming out there if we can't finish the business in the morning as we planned. Hit me up when you get the business done." Then he hung up and dropped his phone unto his lap. He wanted to cuss, but he maintained his composure.

"Are we still going to the airport?" Annabelle asked.

Jamal shot her a look and through clenched teeth he said, "Don't be asking me no dumb ass..." he caught himself and stopped. He was mad, but it wasn't her fault.

With that tone and attitude Annabelle gave him a look and he knew that he should not have reacted like that. Without warning she looked in the rearview mirror, hit her blinker and changed lanes. She exited the expressway.

"What are you doing?" Jamal asked, confused.

Annabelle brought the car to a stop, she put it in park and opened the door, and when she was about to step out, Jamal grabbed her arm. "Belle, what you doing?"

Annabelle didn't respond and yanked her arm away from him, grabbed her purse from the back seat and got out. She slammed the door, cars coming from the off ramp were zipping by. Jamal opened the door on his side and got out and took rapid strides to catch up with Annabelle. He called out her name, but she didn't stop. He caught up to her and grabbed her around her waist and pulled her body into his. In her ear he said, "I'm sorry for snapping, okay? I didn't mean to do that." He tried to lower his tone, making himself sound convincing.

She spun around to face him. Her eyes were fire red, and he knew she was angry as hell. "Is this the way it's gonna be, Jamal?" she spat.

He hugged her tight and held her with his mouth in the crook of her neck. "No, baby, and I'm so sorry." Cars were passing them blowing their horns. Jamal hated to be in a position like that, so he took a deep breath and said, "Please come back to the car. I'm not angry at you, I was angry about the call and I know I should not have talked to you that way."

She shook her head. "No, you should not have and I'm not going to let you talk to me crazy, Jamal."

"Baby, I know; just come on back to the car." She took his hand and they went back to the car. He opened the passenger side door for her and she got in. He went around, got in and adjusted the seat. He looked at her and touched her face gently and she looked at him, her eyes were damp, and his elegant touch made her calm down a little.

"Let's just go home," she said, and he put the car in gear and pulled off. She turned to the window and they rode back to Jamal's house in silence.

8

When they made it home, Annabelle was still giving Jamal the silent treatment. He knew he had to make up for what he had done so he went into romantic mode. After he apologized for the tenth time, Annabelle welcomed his advances and agreed to a candlelit bubble bath. He gave her a glass of wine, while she relaxed in the Jacuzzi tub and he hurried down to prepare dinner. He pulled out the fancy linen, good china and set the table with candles.

Quick, but a delicious dish, he sautéed some salmon, steamed some yellow rice and mixed vegetables. The white wine was chilled in her glass when she came down with her hair pinned up in her bathrobe. He had even lit up a fire in the fireplace and the smooth sounds of R&B was floating through the air.

"Wow, Jamal, this is nice." She smiled. Jamal walked over to her, pulled her in close and kissed her gently on the lips. He took her by the hand and led her to the table and then pulled out her chair. She sat and then he took a seat in the chair on the side of her. The table was massive and to sit across from her would be too big of a distance and he wanted to be close to her.

"All this after our first dispute?" she asked while taking in the romantic scene.

"Yes, I wanted to show you how sorry I am for how I acted."

"Thank you. Your efforts are appreciated, and I accept your apology." Her voice was soft and low.

"Thank you." hHe smiled. "Let's gives thanks," he said, reaching for her hand. She put her hand into his and they bowed their heads. Jamal said a quick prayer over their food and then he said, "Amen."

"Amen."

While they ate, they talked and by the time they were done, Jamal could tell that Annabelle was in a better mood. After they cleared the table and cleaned the kitchen, Jamal asked her, "Would you take a little trip with me? I mean we are packed for the trip we didn't take to Colorado, so we should still get away for the night."

"If you'd like to, I'm in," Annabelle responded.

"Yeah, get dressed, babe, and let me put the bags in the SUV," he said and she went up to change out of her robe. Jamal looked down at his attire and decided he'd change into something else too. He went into his closet and selected a pair of Polo jeans, Polo boots and a red and black lumber jack shirt. He'd told Annabelle to wear something comfortable, so she was dressed in jeans, Nikes and a pullover sweatshirt. Inside the garage they climbed up inside a SUV, and Jamal got behind the wheel. "Have you ever been to the mountains before?" he asked her as he cranked the engine and then hit the button on the garage door opener.

She shook her head and said, "No, I haven't." Then she folded her arms across her chest. "Is that where we're going?"

Jamal backed out the garage and then nodded his head and then glanced over at her.

"I think you'll like it up here."

"I hope so," she said.

"You will," he assured her and before long they were on the

main road. It took them just a little over an hour and a half to reach their destination. Jamal looked around, taking in the scenery. He loved going up to the mountains and he wanted Annabelle to enjoy it too.

"Where are we?" she asked. It was now dark, so he knew she couldn't see much.

"This little town is called Ellijay. I love it out here and every so often I just come out here for a while." Jamal pulled up in a paved half circle driveway and stopped the SUV in front of a cabin. "It's so quiet up here and I love it."

"I can see. I mean the other cabins are like two football fields away from this one. Do you own this place?"

"Yep, it's probably my greatest investment. One of the best things about being up here is you can definitely get a piece of mind. Wait till you see the lake, it's out back. You'll see it in the morning. Trust me, you gonna love this," he said and switched off the engine. "Come on." They got out and he went for the bags in the back. They walked up to the front door, crickets were chirping, frogs were making funny sounds in the night. Jamal put the key in the lock and opened the door. They stepped in and he went for the lights.

"This is beautiful," she said, staring around at the interior.

"Thank you," he said and pulled her into him. She turned around and faced him. They held on to each other for a few moments and Jamal felt their connection and he was feeling good about being with Annabelle and if he wanted to keep her he'd have to find a way to be a better man and treat her right.

"Is there anything to be scared of out there?" Annabelle said, breaking the silence.

"I got you, baby," he said tenderly. The mountain air was thin, and it was cold up there, so Jamal got the fireplace going, while Annabelle changed out of her street clothes. She put on the nightie she had gotten from the mall earlier, but he could see her nipples were rock solid against the fabric and the way she rubbed her arms ever five seconds showed that she was cold. He grabbed an extra blanket and as soon as he handed it to her, she quickly wrapped it around her body.

"Do you want a drink?" he offered.

"Tea would be great. Something warm," she said. He smiled and headed into kitchen. He made them both a cup of tea and added lemon juice, honey and a shot of brandy.

"Here you go, babe," he said and handed her the warm cup of tea. He joined her on the sofa and she let him share her blanket.

She took a sip. "What else did you put in this tea?" she questioned.

"Don't worry, just enjoy it." He smiled. They chatted and finished their tea. He pulled her into his strong arms and it was nice to just hold her. Jamal needed a woman like Annabelle in his life. He was sure she was the one who could motivate him to get his life right.

"So, who decorated this place?"

"I bought it furnished," he said.

"I kinda figured that, because I know you'd never pick this lavender set or that area rug," she joked. The room was gorgeous with floor to ceiling windows on one side and vaulted ceilings. It was cozy enough, but she was right, the furnishings wasn't his true taste, but it was nice enough that he didn't want to give it an overhaul.

"Yeah, you're right, but it's grown on me. Do you like it?"

"I love it," she said.

"Well that means it's perfect," he teased.

She smiled. "I can't believe this is my life now. I mean meeting you wasn't at all what I expected, but God is awesome. I just want us to be happy, Jamal."

"We will be, Annabelle," he assured her and then planted a soft kiss on her lips.

They were quiet and they both peered out the window into the darkness.

"I wonder what animals are lurking out there," Annabelle said, breaking the silence.

"Now, we're up here in the mountains, so we'll probably see a bear or two, but nothing to be alarmed about."

"A bear?" she shrieked. "I'm scared of bears, snakes, lizards, spiders and all creeping things. Everything. I'm not sure if I'll like it up here, baby." She got closer to him and he squeezed her tighter.

Jamal looked at her and touched her underneath her chin with his index finger. "Look at me," he said to her.

Annabelle looked him in his eyes, then he held her face between his hands. "I'll put you on my back and walk through a tunnel of fire to keep you from getting burned."

Annabelle laughed. "Awww that's so sweet. I hear you telling me again that you got me, so I need to just believe it."

"Exactly, now come in the kitchen with me, so I can fix me a drink and make you more tea," he said and stood. He reached for her hand and she took his. They grabbed the empty tea cups from the coffee table and he led the way.

"This place is so lovely, and this kitchen is massive," she said, then added, "Like a picture from a magazine or something."

"This is the only room I had a little work done in. The counters were laminate, so I upgraded to granite, the cabinets were all dark and brown making this room feel like the entire cabin, so they were sanded and painted, and all of the appliance are new. The wood flooring was in perfect condition, so we didn't touch those."

"Well, this kitchen is just as spectacular as the rest of the place. After you showed me to the master and I changed, I looked around and this place is wonderful," she beamed.

"Well, I'm glad you love it, but I have something more to show you upstairs," he said and filled his glass with ice. He poured some Ciroc and didn't add a chaser. "Do you want more tea or a grown-up drink?"

"Tea will be fine, but I don't mind if you spike it." She smiled.

"Yes, just let yourself go, Belle. You need to live a little."

"I know, but I just don't like to indulge in too many things that will interrupt my walk with the Lord," she said.

He nodded as he turned the fire back on under the kettle. "I understand that, baby," he said and went for a tea bag. "This shouldn't take too long to heat up. It's probably still a little warm," he said. They both took a seat at the island and he sipped his drink. When the kettle whistled, he got up to make her tea. With his back to her, he added a little more brandy hat time, and a bit more honey to tone down the taste. He handed it to her.

"Thank you, baby," she said while pulling the cup close to her lips. She blew to cool it and then took her first sip. "Ummmm, that is good. I may need you to make my tea from now on."

"I have no problems with that," he said. They talked and drank and by his second drink, Annabelle was more relaxed and giggling a bit.

"So, are you ready to go upstairs?"

She smiled. "I'm right behind you," she said, and they stood. He led her up a spiral staircase and she followed him to a dark brown wooden door. The door didn't have a knob, but a gray panel was in place of the knob. It was a keypad and he punched in a code and then placed his right thumb over a dark piece of glass until a green light appeared.

The door unlocked and then opened slightly. Jamal pushed the door all the way open and flipped on the light switch. Once Annabelle walked in she looked around in pure amazement. Jamal pressed a button on the wall and the drapes separated giving her a better view. It was dark, but the moon provided enough light for her to see the mountain tops and the lake. The décor was retro, definitely the design of a bachelor's pad, even as over the top as it was, with the two brass lion status on the floor at the foot of the bed, and the black marble floors, she loved the ambiance of it. The lights were dimmed, and the mink blanket over the black satin sheets made her want to climb into his bed. The gold accents gave the room balance, because without it, it would have been too much black for her taste.

"So, this is the true master suite?" she asked.

"It is." He grinned.

"It is amazing and oh, my God, this view is spectacular." Annabelle was in awe. She went over to the large window and just gazed at God's glory. "I've never seen anything this gorgeous in my life." Jamal walked up behind her and wrapped his arms around her and she leaned back and relaxed in his strong powerful arms. At that moment, Annabelle didn't have a care in the world and she exhaled. After what Pastor James and Daisy Mae said earlier about him having a past that wasn't too attractive, she wanted to ask so many questions, but she held her tongue.

"I knew you'd love it," he said.

"I do," she said and then dropped her head.

"What's on your mind, Belle?" he asked. She could see his eyes on her and her expression in their reflection in the glass.

She shrugged her shoulders lightly. "I'm not actually sure how to put into words what I wanna say," she said sadly.

Jamal turned her around to face him. He looked her in the eyes and she knew he was waiting on a straight answer from her.

"I think I'm just a little tired. How about a few minutes of prayer, then some sleep and let's talk tomorrow?"

Jamal gave her a weak smile and she could tell what she had said didn't rest easy with him, but he said, "Cool." He turned and walked over to the bed and sat. Annabelle sat on the bed next to him. She grabbed his hand and said, "Just let Jesus know what's on your mind, it doesn't have to be long, just something quick and simple."

Jamal closed his eyes and said, "God, I'm just trying to do the right thing. I wanna get off these pills. I wanna be successful and have a healthy life and relationship. Will you help me?"

He opened his eyes and looked at Annabelle. She wanted to question him about the pills. *What pills?* She wondered but said nothing. She knew he had demons to fight as all believers in Christ, so she said, "Amen." She wasn't going to judge or condemn, so she didn't say anything else.

Jamal got up and turned off the light in the bedroom and they climbed into bed. She wondered why he didn't remove his clothes, but she didn't ask. Annabelle snuggled up against him and they entwined in one another arms. Jamal kissed her on her forehead. "Good night, Belle," he whispered to her.

"Good night, Jamal," she responded back.

They fell asleep in one another arms.

The following morning, Jamal was up bright and early. He'd crept out of bed and went downstairs to the living room with his phone in hand. He didn't want to wake Annabelle, at least not right then anyway. Walking across the hardwood floors in his socks and his phone pressed up against his face, he said, "Yes, that'll work."

The lady on the other end asked him. "Two hours, correct?"

"That'll work." He was pacing the floor, then he walked over to the window and gazed out at the beautiful views.

"You're all set," she confirmed.

"Thank you." Jamal hung up the phone, and then he walked back upstairs where Annabelle was still sleeping peacefully underneath the comforter. Jamal stood over her and stared at her for a brief moment and then he sat on the bed next to her. He ran the back of his hand along the side of her face until she moaned. Then he leaned down and kissed her on her lips. "Good morning, Belle."

She finally opened her eyes, and when she saw him she smiled. "What time is it?" she asked.

"Time for you to get up, you've been snoring all night and kept me up," he joked, laughing.

Annabelle playfully hit him and said, "I was not snoring." She sat up in the bed and wrapped her arms around his neck and Jamal hugged her back.

"Get yourself together, we bout to go outside," he whispered.

"Outside? And do what, Jamal?" she quizzed.

Jamal pulled her up by her hands, she stood up with him. "Trust me, Belle," he said. "You will like it."

"I better." She smiled.

"You will, and I brought your bags up."

"Thanks," she said and then she headed into the bathroom and closed the door behind her.

Jamal was standing there waiting for her. He rubbed his hands together anxiously.

"Now, that's what I'm talking about," he said.

"What?"

"You're just so beautiful."

She blushed. "Thank you."

"You ready?" he asked her.

"I guess."

They went downstairs, and Jamal had already had coffee brewing. He filled the two mugs with the liquid caffeine and after Annabelle added her creamer and sugar, they popped the lids on top and went outside. The wind was blowing, but it wasn't as cold as Jamal thought it would be. Jamal held Annabelle's hand as he guided her up a winding dirt road. They walked and talked and sipped their coffee and Annabelle would stop to take in the different views.

"It has to be spooky out here at night," she said.

Jamal held her hand tightly as they trekked through the rocks and branches. When they made it passed the uneven ground they were greeted by a tall older man. He was in the path, standing there as if he was taking a break. His hair and beard were white as snow and his eyes were green as emeralds. They were a bit sunk in, but that was because he was well up in age.

Dressed in denim jeans, a matching jacket and cowboy boots, he looked pretty healthy at his age.

"Mr. Pete," Jamal smiled and extended his hand. "It's good to see you again."

Mr. Pete nodded his head. "Jamal, how you doing? It's been awhile since you been up in these parts," he returned with a heavy southern drawl. He gave Jamal a firm handshake and then he extended his hand to Annabelle and they shook.

"Good morning, young lady," he said to her.

"Good morning, Mr. Pete, my name is Annabelle," she greeted him with a charming smile.

"Nice to meet you, Annabelle. You two, come on and follow me," he said and turned towards the other direction. Mr. Pete walked fast, and they followed him over to a huge wooden stable and he pulled the door open. Inside were eight well-groomed horses, each in the their own stable. "Is this your first-time riding," he asked, looking at Annabelle.

She nodded. "Why yes sir it is, and I had no idea I'd be riding a horse today."

"Surprise!" Jamal smiled.

"So, we're about to go horseback riding?" she asked Jamal.

"Yes, but if don't want to we can just go back and chill."

"No, I'd love to try it," she said, "I've always wanted to do this. I mean, I'm all for trying new things."

Jamal took her coffee mug and sat them on a counter. He made a mental note of what she had said, because there were several new things he wanted to introduce her to. That little get away is not only what he needed, but he could tell she needed it too. Mr. Pete pulled out a beautiful chestnut colored horse with big bright eyes. He was more of a copper tone than brown, with white markings on his head and underneath his neck, but beautiful none the less.

Annabelle's eyes widened. "I've never been up this close to a horse before," she said excitedly. She walked up to the horse and rubbed his right side. He made a small sound with his mouth when she touched him, and she wore a huge smile. Jamal walked up next to her and patted the horse and then he grabbed the reigns and pulled him towards the entrance door. And he and Mr. Pete gave her some quick instructions, he helped Annabelle get up on the horse back and she got comfortable on the saddle. She smiled down at Jamal and said, "I'm ready."

"Stay right here, my horse should be out here in a moment." Jamal said, and Mr. Pete walked out the horse that he would be riding. That one was reddish brown with a black mane, and a small patch of white on top of his head. Jamal reached in his pocket and pulled out a folded knot of money and peeled off three one hundred-dollar bills and handed them to Mr. Pete. Even though the ride wasn't that much but he always tipped the old man extra. When Mr. Pete handed him the straps, Jamal said, "We'll be back in about an hour."

Mr. Pete nodded his head. "Take your time, Jamal, and you two have fun."

Jamal and Annabelle took off at a slow steady pace with the horses walking next to one another. The expression on Annabelle's face said it all and he knew that it was a good idea to take her riding.

"Now, this is fun and relaxing," she said while smiling and nodding his head.

"I was hoping that you would like it."

"Jamal, come on, this is like the perfect date, so thank you."

He smiled. "You're most welcome."

They rode along the wooded trails, and they enjoyed the fresh air and glorious scenery. Birds were chirping and singing from a distance in the trees. It was silence between the both of them at times as they rode, but not weird silence. Jamal felt his phone vibrating in his pocket, and he paused to retrieve it. He looked at the screen and the name Kia was on it. She was one of his clients, so he took the call.

"No more than an hour, the door is open," he replied. He then ended the call and looked over at Annabelle. She was just riding, relaxing and enjoying nature. *Life couldn't be any better than that moment for them,* he thought.

"Look at this, Jamal, this right here," she said, outstretching her arm towards the sky.

"This right here confirms that there is a God," she glowed. Jamal smiled back at her, because he did like seeing her happy. If only she wasn't Godly, he said and then said. No, that's what he needed, because Annabelle and God were what he needed if he truly wanted to change.

Jamal extended his hand out to her.

"Come on, babe, let's head back," he said.

She pulled the straps and the horse trotted back over to Jamal. She took his hand.

"This was so nice. I had a wonderful morning. I mean this is like the most romantic outing I've ever been on."

Jamal nodded his head and said, "Oh, this is just the beginning, baby." He squeezed her hand, and then kissed the back of it. The smile on her face was wider than the lake behind his cabin and he knew she was falling for him. It was written all over her face.

9

When they returned to the cabin Annabelle was floating. She was falling head over heels for Jamal and she was excited to see just how far their relationship would go. There was no turning back and she wanted to be with him and she was sure he wanted to be with her.

As soon as they got to the door, it opened, and Annabelle jumped, but she then noticed his jacket and hat. He wore a white chef's coat and chef's hat. His face was clean with a neatly trimmed beard, sitting on top of his smooth bronze complexion.

"Good morning and welcome home. I am Chef Daniel," he greeted them with a gorgeous smile and reached for Annabelle's hand first.

"Good morning, I'm Annabelle." She smiled and then shook his outstretched hand.

"Good morning," Jamal returned when he shook his hand.

"Come on in you two," he said, clearing the entryway. They both followed him inside. "Breakfast will be ready in a few moments. Today, I will be serving T-Bone steaks, eggs over easy, pecan pancakes, mixed berries and the best mimosas you've ever tasted in your life," he said confidently.

"Oh wow, that's sounds delicious," Annabelle said and rubbed her tummy.

"Yes, it does," Jamal added.

"Well, whenever you are ready, the dining table is already set for you." With that he headed back to the kitchen.

"Oh, my God, a gourmet breakfast, Jamal! How? I mean when?" she asked shaking her head.

Jamal smiled and shrugged his shoulders, and said, "Only the best for you. I keep telling you that I'm going to take care of you and I don't know any woman that doesn't want to be treated to the best."

She beamed. "You are absolutely right, and you are doing an awesome job spoiling me. I mean I've never been treated like this. God is so good to me."

"No, God is good to us," he said and reached for her hands. She put her hands into his and he pulled her in for a kiss.

"Let's go and take our seats at the table because the aroma of that food is driving me insane," she suggested.

"Let's go," he agreed, and they headed to the dining room table. He pulled out Annabelle's chair and she sat. He took the seat near her, where the other place setting was.

"This morning has been perfect, Jamal. First, the horseback riding, and then having our own personal chef cook us breakfast. What's next, mister?"

"Well, a little later on today I have a couple coming here to give us full body massages. They should be here about two," he informed her and then Chef Daniel approached the table with a cart with their plates of hot food. He presented Annabelle with her dishes first and then Jamal. Everything looked delicious and Annabelle was ready to dig in.

"Wow, Chef Daniel, this plate looks amazing. I mean, it's so gorgeously decorated with these beautiful colors of garnishes, I don't want to mess it up," Annabelle giggled.

"Thank you, Annabelle, and trust me it tastes just as good as it looks," Chef Daniel said.

"I bet," Jamal added.

"I have a pitcher of mimosas made up for you two. I'll be back to fill your glasses," he said and then turned to head back into the kitchen. He was back in a flash and filled their glasses.

"Please, enjoy your breakfast," he said and turned to walk away, but Annabelle stopped him.

"Chef Daniel, can you please tell me why our mimosas are pinkish?" she asked.

He chuckled. "Because I always add orange juice and cranberry juice to my mimosas, go ahead, try it," he suggested.

Annabelle lifted the glass to her lips and took a sip. "Oh, my Lord this is good," she said.

"I told you," he winked and then vacated the room.

"Now grace," Jamal said and reached for Annabelle's hand.

She took it. "May I?" she asked, and he nodded yes. They bowed their heads.

"Father, thank you for this wonderful breakfast that we're about to receive, and bless this food to fuel our bodies with nourishments. We pray that we will be energized and be able to work for the glory of your kingdom. In Jesus name, Amen."

"Amen." Jamal said and smirked at her. "One thing for sure, you got a prayer for everything, huh?"

Annabelle picked up her knife and fork and began cutting into her pancakes that were covered with pecans and melting butter. "You can never go wrong with prayer, Jamal. Look at how blessed we are, so all we have to do is open our mouths and give Jesus a little praise."

Jamal nodded his head up and down. He grabbed his utensils and went straight for his steak and said, "I definitely feel you on that."

❧

Sunday came back around fast, and Pastor James was standing in the pulpit with a microphone pinned on his jacket. From where he was standing, he saw that his congregation was growing, and it felt good to see so many new faces. He noticed Annabelle and his brother were sitting in the third row. He hadn't seen his brother in church that much since they were kids. "Glory to God this morning," his voice boomed through the speakers throughout the church. Everybody in the pews started to clap and some of the women stood up on their feet and raised their hands. "Thank you, Jesus. Praise the Lord, glory to God," were some of the chants that were coming from the members. Pastor James had his hands on his waist as he paced the floor from back to forward and looked out at the audience. "God answer all prayers. He may not answer them when you want him to, but He most certainly will answer them when you need Him to."

"Amen." A female voice came from the front row.

Pastor James looked at her and nodded, and then his eyes went to Annabelle for a brief moment. He had hoped that the smile she wore was because she was truly happy, because he still had doubts that Jamal had completely changed. He then quickly cut his eyes at his brother who was also smiling, but he knew Jamal's smile could be deceiving at times and he continuously prayed to God for him to deliver his brother from his sinful ways. He also prayed for Annabelle, because she was a humble woman and a man like Jamal wasn't the best fit for her. He put his focus back on the congregation and then went back to his opened bible that was on top of the podium. He looked down at it, studied the pages for a second and then he looked back up at the hearers of the messages from God. "I'm reading from Matthew this morning, chapter five, verse forty-four. But I say unto you, love your enemies, bless them that curse you, do good to them that hate you, and pray for them which despitefully use you, and persecute you." He paused and took a deep breath, and then his head began moving side to side. Pastor James smiled and looked out at his people. "Now, when I first read that message from the Bible I had to pray to God for more understanding. Love my enemies?" he questioned with a look of confusion. "Me personally, I was like, I don't know about that one God," he joked and then laughed lightly.

A few laughs and Amens came from the onlookers. "No seriously, you couldn't have told me to pray for Lil Mike, the dude that gave me a black eye when I was in middle school. My own mama didn't teach me to pray for him. I had to fight that little devil every day. Then he was shorter than me, but that rascal was tougher than nails."

More laughter came from the audience.

"I most definitely didn't want to pray for the dude that loved beating me up. Well, I might have prayed one time, but that was for him to leave me alone," he laughed, and most of the congregation laughed with him. "Prayer transforms us, and we can grow to love our enemies as we love our own family members. It's the work of the Holy Spirit. Give God what He wants, and He will give you what you want. Can I get an amen?" he said.

The entire church began to applaud and shout.

*

JAMAL FELT HIS PHONE VIBRATE, SO HE PULLED IT FROM HIS SUIT jacket pocket. He swiped the screen and keyed in his code and went to the text. It read, I NEED 2 C U TDY. IT'S IMPORTANT. I need to see you today, it's important. Jamal hated messages like that, especially when they came from females that he'd dealt with in the past. He texted her back, I'M IN CHURCH RIGHT NOW & I DIDN'T DRIVE. I'LL COME BY IN A COUPLE OF HOURS. He hit send and when he got the READ notification he was about to put his phone away, but she replied, THAT LIL PRETTY RED CHICK GOT U THAT F'ED UP THAT U CAN'T GIVE ME A FEW MINUTES OF UR TIME. Not happy at all with her response, Jamal texted back, EXACTLY! Then he eased his phone back into his suit pocket, and then he looked over at Annabelle. She had her eyes closed and her head down, then he noticed that the entire church had their heads bowed in prayer. He bowed his head and began to pray as well, as he listened to his brother's voice pray through the speakers. He was saying a prayer for the entire church. After the prayer was over, the ushers collected the tithes and offerings and then came the benediction. Jamal reached over and grabbed Annabelle's hand and kissed her cheek. "You ready to head home?" he asked.

She smiled and nodded and gave him a yes.

✃

OUTSIDE IN THE PARKING LOT, ANNABELLE WAS WALKING TO THE driver side of the Porsche and Jamal was going to the passenger side. When she got to the door, she opened it and got in. She removed her purse from her shoulder and pulled her cellphone out and sat it in the cup holder. Annabelle started the car just as Jamal was getting in. Her phone whistled, indicating that she had a text message. She picked up her phone and pressed the message icon and there was a text and a video messaged attached. Annabelle quickly read the text before pressing play.

TELL JAMAL SINCE HE WANNA PLAY, I'M GOING TO PLAY 2. That confused her, she bunched her eyebrows together and hit the play button and then her phone went dead. She pressed a few buttons trying to get her phone to power back on, but nothing worked. She looked over at Jamal, then her eyes scanned the middle console of the car and the front seat floor. When she didn't see what she was looking for she asked, "Have you seen my charger?" The tone of her voice had changed a little, nearly at a high pitch.

"Nah, babe, was it in here?" Jamal looked over at her and responded.

"Yes, I mean, I'm not sure if I left it in your SUV when I drove it yesterday," she said continuing to look around for it. It was clear she didn't have it, so she gave up looking and looked at Jamal. "Someone just texted me with a number I didn't recognize with a message for you," she said and gave him the look showing she wasn't too happy.

"What? What message? What are you talking about?" he questioned, holding his facial expression as serious as possible.

"Before my stupid phone died, I got a text saying to tell you since you wanna play, I'm going to play, too. There was a video message there, but my phone died before I could view it."

Jamal looked at her innocently and then he shrugged his shoulders. "Probably somebody playing, I'm not sure."

"Really, Jamal?" she challenged.

"Yes, really. It's a Walmart right around the corner if you wanna grab a charger," he said and kind of shrugged it off.

"I don't really want to buy another charger, so can you check the backseat and floor. If it's not there, I'll wait until we get home."

Jamal looked between the seats and then felt around to the backseat floor. "I don't see it, babe."

"Thanks. I'll just wait until we get home," she said with an attitude.

She knew it was more to that text, she could feel it in her bones and she couldn't wait to get to the house, so she could watch that video. She started the car and then it hit her that her charger was in her purse. She dug in her purse and retrieved it. "Here it is," she said.

"You got it?"

"Yes, I do," she said and then plugged it in. She plugged the cord into her phone, but it was so dead that it didn't power back on right away, so she put it down.

"We gon' sit here for a minute and see what else is in this phone, since you say you don't know."

"I don't, and this can really wait until we get home, baby," he said.

She eyed him trying to see if she could see panic, but Jamal played it cool, his demeanor was always smooth and easy. "Nah, as soon as this phone powers back on...," she was saying then there was a knock on the window. She turned to see it was Daisy Mae. Annabelle rolled down her window.

"Sister Daisy Mae, what's wrong?" Annabelle asked.

"I'm so glad I caught you before you left. I need you to come back in and get the bags for the crafts you're going to work on this week for the kids next Sunday. You forgot them in the classroom."

Annabelle tapped her forehead. "I sure did," she said and then let up her window. Daisy Mae stepped back and then Annabelle opened her door and got out. She and Daisy Mae headed back into the church.

&

AS SOON AS ANNABELLE WAS ON THE OTHER SIDE OF THE DOOR, Jamal snatched up her phone and was thanking God it had enough juice to power on. Once the phone was completely up, he went straight to her messages and deleted the message. He looked at the church doors to see if Annabelle was coming, and he was relieved to not see her.

He powered off her phone and then put it back down. He let out a deep breath and was glad he had got rid of the message, because there was no telling what was in that video message. Pissed at the fact she had done that dumb stuff, he pulled out his phone and went to his messages and begin typing as fast as his fingers could move.

SHAWTY IF U WANNA PLAY WITH ME TEXT MY WOMAN AGAIN & U GON' C HOW I GET DOWN!

He looked at his phone and sure enough Crazy replied with a middle finger emoji. He shook his head and then saw Annabelle was headed back towards the car. She opened the door and hit the button to open the trunk. She put the bags in and then she slammed the truck shut. He knew it was going to be some words exchanged, but he was prepared, because he knew she'd have a mouth full once she discovered the message was deleted.

She got in and he thought she'd just pull out, but she immediately went for her phone. Jamal braced himself for her outburst, but he was cool with it. He'd rather her fuss about the messaged getting deleted than to possibly leave him after seeing whatever evil the other women sent to her. He watched as she powered it on and didn't say a word.

A moment or two later, she shot him a look that was cold, her eyes were slits.

"You deleted the message, didn't you?" she roared.

"I didn't touch yo' phone," he lied, holding up his hand in mock surrender.

"You're lying," she yelled.

"Look, baby, I don't need no drama with no ex interrupting our good thing, so yes, I deleted it. It's childish and petty," he said. He hoped she'd let it go without making a bigger deal about it, so he added, "You're the only woman for me, babe, and you know this, so please don't be mad and don't let Satan set you up to lose the good thing God has given you."

She rolled her eyes at him. "I'm not going to trouble myself over it. All I ask of you is that you keep me out of your drama. I didn't sign up for that mess, so whatever you got going on with that woman that texted me, you need to handle it," she spat.

Without another word, she threw the car in gear and backed out of the parking space. She peeled out of the church parking lot and the tires screeched on the asphalt. At the moment, all he did was shake his head, pressed the seat recliner button on the passenger seat and leaned back and closed his eyes. For the next twenty minutes, Jamal's mind was racing in several different directions and to the point that it actually had him feeling uncomfortable. When they pulled up in the driveway of the house, Annabelle pressed the button on the garage door opener and pulled up in the middle bay. Then she pressed it again for it to close behind her. After she put the car in park, she shut off the engine.

She grabbed her phone and purse and went in the house, leaving Jamal in the car. Jamal took a deep breath, then opened the door and got out and headed inside with thoughts of how to make things right again with Annabelle. He'd have to go back into romance mode, but if that's what it was going to take, he'd do it. When he got to the side door and walked inside the house he went into the kitchen where Annabelle was standing at plugging in her phone. Jamal stood on the other side of the island, folded his arms and just stared at her, but she didn't look back at him. Annabelle was now holding the power button, anxiously waiting for it to turn on.

Jamal went over to his wet bar that was off from the kitchen and made himself a drink. He grabbed a bottle of Patron silver and removed the cork while shaking his head. When he started pouring the liquor into a glass, Annabelle just stomped by him and headed up the stairs. Jamal threw back a double shot with no chaser, and the liquor burned as it went down. He frowned and looked to make sure Annabelle had gone up the stairs.

She did.

He pulled out his phone, it was flooded with text messages and all of them were from the same person. Kia, pronounced just like the car. Jamal called her number and she answered on the third ring. "Shawty, you trippin' and you really need to fall back."

"Nigga, don't ever try to play me like that; I already sent your girl a clip of the video that you wanted recorded."

"Are you high? Every time you get on them Adderall pills and Xanax you start trippin'. I'll be over there in a few minutes," he barked and then he hit the end button. He put his glass down and moved to the stairs. He was about to head up to go and talk to her, but he saw her standing at the top of the stairs looking down at him. She had tears rolling down her face and she just shook her head at him.

"So.... you just... let someone... record us having sex, Jamal?"

"Come again?" he said because he knew he hadn't said those words and it was impossible for Annabelle to hear Kat on the other end.

"You heard me," she yelled.

Still lost he said, "Belle, what in the hell are you talking about?" His heart was racing, because for her to say those words that meant she knew something.

"Your whore sent me another message," she screeched and then pressed play. She held up her phone and all he heard was the moans and groans that belonged to him and her, and at that given moment he could have dropped dead.

10

*J*amal was looking up at Annabelle, holding her phone. He knew he'd kill Kat for sure now for resending that video. The plan was to record them having a threesome, but since that hadn't gone down, he didn't know she still recorded him and Annabelle and he then hated that he had given her access to the camera and the code to access it. He was screwed for sure and he had no idea how he was going to talk his way out of that one, so the first words that sprung from his tongue was the truth. Annabelle would only listen if he told her the truth, because he had no idea that she actually recorded them.

"Belle, listen to me. I had no idea she made that video, I swear!" he pleaded in his best tone of voice.

"Lies!" she blasted angrily and ran down the steps. As soon as she hit the bottom she got in his face, nearly nose to nose. "I don't believe you, Jamal, and after you tried to set me up to sleep with another woman, I should have known you were up to no good."

"Annabelle, you know that's not me. I didn't set you up, that was all her doing, not me. She sold me on some therapeutic BS and my plans were just to show you a good time," he said. That time he lied, because he had every intention on having them both, and showing Annabelle how he loved to get down.

Annabelle shook her head. "I don't believe a word coming from your mouth and I'm done," she declared and then she tried to storm away, but he grabbed her arm. She tried to slap his face, but he leaned back quickly, and her slap didn't connect.

"Let me go now," she wailed, but he refused to release her.

"Please Belle," he pleaded, and pulled her body into his. He locked his arms around her waist.

She squirmed and cried for him to release her, but it was useless, and he only tightened his hold. "Jamal, I'm begging you to let me go. I can't stay with you anymore. I wanna leave," she cried, but her tears didn't motivate him to cooperate.

"You're not going anywhere until you calm down and we can talk," he said through clenched teeth.

"Talk? Talk?" she yelled at him. "There is nothing we need to talk about," she barked.

"You the one that said God brought us together, right?"

"Don't you dare try to put God's name in this madness. Now, let me go, Jamal."

Jamal finally let go of her. Annabelle took a few deep breaths and then went to the message on her phone. "You think I have anything to say other than goodbye after seeing this?" she snared and then hit play again. That angered him, so he snatched the phone from her hand and slammed it on the wooden floor. She went to grab it, but he kicked it across the room.

"You know what! Have it!" she spat and then ran up the stairs. Jamal was right behind her. "You ain't leaving, Belle," he shouted to her back.

"Oh, yes, the hell I am!" she fired back.

"Can we sit down and talk about this?" He watched as Annabelle snatched open the closet door and began to remove some of her clothes. She paused and then walked into the other closet and grabbed a large suitcase and flung it on the plush bench that was at the foot of his Cali king bed. "Please, just talk to me," he begged.

"I'm done talking to you Jamal," she hissed. He was not trying to watch her leave so he grabbed her and tried to stop her again and grabbed her by the wrist.

"Stop it," she bellowed.

He released her wrist and then thought of another way to handle her. He knew Annabelle and he knew how he could get her to calm down, so he said, "Listen, I'll let you leave, okay? I'll get you over to Daisy Mae's and let you calm down and then we can talk."

"You can get me to Daisy Mae's, but I can assure you that I'm not ever coming back to you." She unzipped the bag and started to throw her things into the bag. Jamal vacated the room and then went downstairs. He went into the kitchen and grabbed the tea kettle and filled it halfway with water and put it on the burner. He grabbed her favorite thermal from the cabinet and her herbal tea. Took a pill from the bottle he had tucked in the back of one of the kitchen drawers and crushed it. He put the contents in her teabag and when the kettle whistled, he poured the hot water in. He added five heaping teaspoons of honey and grabbed a fresh lemon from the fridge and sliced it into wedges and squeezed two of the wedges into the thermo. He gave it a few stirs and then took a quick sip. When he couldn't taste the medicine, he smiled and twisted on the lid. He ran back up and offered Annabelle help with her bag, and she didn't even look at him.

He grabbed her bag and then went down before her. When she came down, he handed her the tea. "Here, I made you some herbal tea, to help calm your nerves."

She paused and then took the thermo. "Now, let's go," she ordered. They got into his SUV and he looked over at her and said, "I'm really sorry, Belle."

"Yes, you are," she shot back.

"Just talk to me. I don't want it to end," he tried to say, but she threw up a hand.

"Don't," she said. He hit the garage opener and then started the engine. He was happy to see her take her first sip before he had backed out. Not even halfway to Daisy Mae's house, Annabelle rested her head back and yawned. She kept drinking tea and when she put the thermo into the cup holder he knew she'd be out soon. He kept looking over at her as her eyes grew heavy, but she continued to fight it. Before he turned onto Daisy Mae's street she was out. He pulled over and said, "Annabelle," but she didn't respond. He shook her, but she didn't open her eyes. He undid his seatbelt, got out and then he went around and opened her door. He hit the button on her side to recline her seat.

He got back in, made a U-Turn and headed up to the mountains. He smiled at his plans to keep Annabelle up there until he made peace with her and then thought back on the events of the night that had him and his lady ending before they could barely get started.

They were at the cabin in the mountains and Jamal arranged for two of his lady friends to come over and give them both a full body massage. Kat and her associate, Melanie, had gone to the cabin together, but Kat stayed behind after Melanie made her departure. When the two arrived and Jamal opened the door, he admired them both. Kat was stunning and although Melanie was a very attractive woman, Kat's sculpted body looked like a piece of art. She was Brazilian and Cuban mixed, and her golden skin tone glowed. Her hair was long and silky, and she had honey brown eyes that a man could get lost in.

"Come on in, ladies," Jamal grinned. He closed the door and took pleasure in eyeing Kat up and down. Both ladies wore dark yoga pants, long-sleeved dark V-necks and tennis shoes, but Kat looked good in whatever she sported, and Jamal admired her backside and her curves.

"Thank you, ladies, for coming all the way up here to service me and my lady on short notice," he said and showed them to the sofa. "You ladies can have a seat," he offered.

Kat and Melanie took a seat and then he offered them something to drink. They both declined, and Annabelle walked into the room. When Kat saw her, she smiled and stood up. "Well, this must be the beautiful, Annabelle, that I have been hearing so much about." *She extended her hand out to her.*

Annabelle shook her hand. "Yes, I am Annabelle, and you?"

"I'm Kat and this is Melanie. We will be your personal massage therapists for today. We are going to make you and Jamal wonderful and relaxed for a nice long hour."

Annabelle smiled at the young beauty and then looked at Jamal. "I thought you said a couple?" *she asked.*

"I'm sorry, I just meant a couple of masseuses." *He smiled and shrugged his shoulders.*

"Well, I guess I'm ready to get started."

"Perfect," *Kat said.* "We just need to go out to the truck and get our tables and oils. Where should we set up?"

"I guess near the windows, so you ladies can enjoy the spectacular view while you work," *Jamal suggested.*

"That's fine," *Melanie said. They both headed for the door, but Melanie paused and said,* "You two may wanna undress and grab your robes. We can't massage you two fully dressed."

"Indeed," *Jamal said. The two walked out the door, leaving Annabelle and Jamal alone in the living room.*

"Jamal, I'm so excited," *Annabelle expressed.*

"You should be. Today is going to be a special day for you and me both." *He grinned.*

"I hope so," *she beamed.* Let's got undressed," *she said, and he followed her up. They both came back down in their robes and the two young ladies were finishing their set up. After the tables were up, aroma heat lamps were lit, Annabelle and Jamal took their positions on the tables. They exchanged romantic banter as the two women went to work. When the timer buzzed, Annabelle felt relaxed and she silently thanked God for that body therapy.*

They packed up and toted their equipment back to their vehicle, and Annabelle said her goodbyes before heading up to run her a hot bath.

Jamal walked them out and he paid Melanie and assured her that Kat would call her when she needed to be picked up. Jamal had gotten them a room at the local inn and since Melanie wasn't down for the games Jamal and Kat wanted to play, she took her cash and bounced. Kat retrieved her bag before Melanie pulled away and then she and Jamal headed back inside.

"Where is Annabelle?" Kat asked.

"She went up for a bath," Jamal said.

"Perfect!" She smiled. She put her bag on the sofa and unzipped it. Jamal headed to the kitchen to pour them a glass of champagne.

"We're celebrating today, baby, all day," he said as he opened the fridge. He was about to introduce Annabelle to something new and he hoped she'd just get loose and give him a chance to show her what true pleasure was about.

"Yes, she has to learn what real pleasure is," he said and then went for the champagne glasses.

He was anxious to get things started and he swore that his plan would come off without a hitch. He pulled his iPhone from his pocket and then pressed a couple of buttons until the hidden cameras upstairs in the bedroom showed on his screen. He saw Annabelle getting undressed and he smiled. When she headed into the bathroom, he popped the bottle and poured three glasses. He was sure to put another bottle in the fridge to chill and then he headed back to the living room. He handed Kat a glass and then said," Let me go up and tell Annabelle that there is something extra in this massage treatment and I'll let you know when to come in," he said.

She smiled. "Okay baby. I'm ready to make the both of you feel good," she purred and walked closer into Jamal's space. She ran her tongue across his lips and with her free hand she grabbed his semi erection.

"Damn baby, you're making me hard," he said, because within seconds he was rock hard.

"That's what you're paying me for. I mean, this lifestyle never gets old and I'm ready to play with your new church girl," she hissed.

"Well, you know what to do, on my cue," he said and then backed away. He went up with two glasses of champagne and Annabelle was laid back in the tub soaking. "Here you go my love," he said, and she opened her eyes.

"Thanks baby, this is like the best day ever."

"And there is more," he said.

Her eyes widened. "More?" she questioned. "What else can top this?" she asked.

"You will see, and Belle I want you to keep an open mind baby," he said.

"Jamal, what are you up to?" she asked.

"Just stay right here and there is more pleasure to come. Kat is here to stimulate your body more," he said.

"Say what?" she questioned with her brows furrowed.

"Shhhhh, come on, baby. You said you were open to try new things and I want to show you some new things," he said. The look on Annabelle's face was of a naïve church girl and he wanted to break that shell.

"I'm not sure what you have in mind, but if it involves the stimulation she put on my body earlier, I'm in."

A devilish grin spread across his face. He went and called for Kat and she walked in with a tray of goodies.

"Hi Annabelle," she cooed.

"Kat," Annabelle said with a nod.

Kat put her tray down on the vanity between the double sinks and then picked up a bottle. "Now, I know this is all new to you, so my advice to you is to just relax and let me make you feel good."

With that, Jamal backed away and went for his pills. He tuned his phone into the hidden camera in the bathroom and watched the screen closely. Jamal removed two Xanax pills, one Adderall and popped the three of them in his mouth at the same time. Then he washed them down with the golden fluids from his champagne. He watched intensely *as Kat touched and caressed Annabelle's skin. Annabelle sipped her drink and then rested and let Kat massage her body in the water. Kat paused, and stood and began to undress. Annabelle's eyes were shut and when she opened them and saw Kat in a laced bra and panty set, there was a look of shock and panic plastered on Annabelle's face.*

He watched the two exchange words and he polished off his drink. The exchange looked a bit heated and the champagne wasn't enough to kick in the feeling that Jamal needed to go and diffuse the situation, so he put the champagne flute on the island and made his was over to the bar. He poured a double shot of Hennessy Black and threw it back. After two more, he rushed back over to his phone to see what the ladies were doing before he headed up. He wanted to have them both and wanted Annabelle to be a willing participant, but he had a strong feeling that the night would be a disaster.

When he saw that Kat was in the water with Annabelle, he figured Kat had handled the situation. She was behind Annabelle, massaging her neck and Jamal smiled. Whatever Kat said to relax Belle worked, because his plans were still in motion. His pills were starting to take effect and the shots he took had him right, so he poured champagne in his flute and headed upstairs.

"Baby, hi you feeling so far?" Jamal asked her.

"It's so relaxing, baby; it feels wonderful." Annabelle said, her eyes were closed, and Kat looked up at him seductively.

"After she finishes in here I'll let her lay you down and then give you the hot rocks."

"Oh, you got the hot rocks also?" Annabelle asked.

"I do and as I told you, it's all about you today. What's a thera-peutic massage without the hot rocks?"

"Right," Jamal agreed. "I'm going in the bedroom and relax until you two get there." He leaned down and kissed Annabelle on her lips and gave Kat a small peck on her cheek. Then he turned and walked out the door.

Without another word, Kat just worked her hands-on Annabelle's neck and shoulders and relaxed her. Then she leaned down to her ear and whispered. "How you feeling?"

"Good, really good," she mumbled.

Kat then moved her hands down to the top of her breast. Annabelle tensed up, but Kat relaxed her. "I'm not going to hurt you, baby, all I need you to do is to relax for me," Kat coached and then she moved her hands over both of her nipples.

"I'm not sure if I want to continue this," Annabelle said softly.

And with that being said, Kat moved her hands from her breast, she then stood up. She got out of the tub and said, "I was just doing what I was told, sweetheart. Massaging your breast is part of a full body massage." She then reached for Annabelle's hand. Annabelle took it and then got out of the tub.

"You really don't know how lucky and blessed you are, let me tell you something about this dude, Jamal, that's madly in love with you. He can basically have any woman in Atlanta that he wants and some kind of way he fell for you. Take advantage of it because its big competition out here."

Annabelle grabbed her towel and covered herself.

"I understand where you coming from, Kat, but when God has his hands in it, there can never be any competition."

Kat didn't like that statement at all, she smiled and didn't argue. "Now, I like that, Boo," she said. She dressed as quickly as she could and then she turned around and opened the door. Jamal was in the middle of the bed only in a robe. He sat up in the bed when he heard the door open. "What's wrong, Belle?" he asked. She was standing behind a fully dressed Kat.

Annabelle didn't answer right away. She just walked over and stood near the bed. Kat stood frozen. "I'm not sure what you thought, but I'm just not feeling this situation at all."

Jamal didn't even say a word, he just grabbed her hand and pulled on it.

"Kat, show yourself out, so I can talk to Jamal," she said, and the

other woman exited the room. Annabelle climbed into the bed with him,
he wrapped his arms around her and started kissing her.

∾

KAT LEFT THE ROOM, BUT SHE PULLED OUT HER PHONE AND WENT TO
the app that Jamal told her to download on her phone. She watched as
they kissed, and he touched Annabelle's body. She was turned on and
wanted to finish what she had started and get what she came for. She
hit record, put her phone down and then she went into the kitchen to fix
a drink. Her glass was still upstairs, but a glass was on the island, so
she filled it. She peeped at the camera and went to her bag and decided
to just take it upstairs. She had toys and gadgets, so that was going to
be her last attempt to please them and have the orgasms she had been
waiting to have all afternoon. When she walked back into the room,
Annabelle was laying on top of Jamal, and she thought she may have
fallen asleep. She crept into the bathroom and got her empty glass and
then eased back down the stairs. She refilled it and then went into her
front pocket and removed a small capsule of Rohypnol. In the streets, it
was called Roofies, a well-known date rape drug and it was perfect for
her plans. She pulled it open and dumped it in the drink that was for
Annabelle and said to herself. "Ain't no church broad about to take my
man!" And then she went back up the steps and pretended to offer up
apologies. She thought that would give her an opportunity to get what
she came for, but Annabelle wasn't having it. She took the glass sat it
down and ordered her to leave. When Jamal didn't come to her defense,
she just put her glass down and left. She waited outside on the porch for
Melanie to pick her up, but she watched the cameras. Annabelle drank
her drink and moments later, she watched Annabelle and Jamal have
sex. She smiled, because although she didn't participate, she had
footage, just enough ammo to get anything she wanted from her
and Jamal.

11

*W*hen Annabelle opened her eyes, it took her all of five seconds to realize that Jamal had taken her back to the mountains. She was in the same lake house where all the mess had started in the first place and she became sick to her stomach. Sitting up in the bed, she tried to remember the events before she woke up and after a few short moments it hit her. "The damn tea," she said and leaped from the bed to go and find him. She raced down the steps and he was chilling on the sofa like he hadn't kidnapped her.

"What the hell, Jamal? Are you outta your damn mind?"

He stood and turned to her. "Belle, baby, calm down," he said gently.

"I will not calm down, Jamal, and there is no way I'm staying here with you," she said and tried to race for the door, but he moved like the flash of lightening and blocked her path.

"Listen here woman," he said between clenched teeth and pointed a finger in her face. "I am tired of your ungrateful behind acting like I did you wrong."

"Oh, so I'm ungrateful now!" she said with a look of terror on her face. She had seen Jamal act up before, but the current Jamal was a different kinda crazy. To drug her and take her miles from civilization was making her more terrified of him than she had ever been.

"Yes, and you are going to cut out all of this craziness and work this out with me and I'm not letting you leave until we are back on track."

She shook her head. "No, Jamal, you can't keep me here. It won't change anything," she assured him.

"Well, I guess you've underestimated me then, because I'm never letting go." He had an evil look in his eyes when he said that, followed by the heavy breathing didn't make it no better.

"Pastor James was right to warn me about you. I should have listened to him," Annabelle growled.

"I don't give a damn what Pastor James said. Pastor James ain't the one got you riding around here in a Porsche or sleeping good every night in six thousand square feet of Buckhead luxury. And he damn sho' ain't the one that got you with an unlimited Black card," her roared, getting her face.

She trembled and took a step back. "Jamal, this is insane and if you just take me back, I promise on my life that I won't tell anyone. You don't even have to take me, I'll find help, just please, let me leave," she cried.

"Negative, now Daniel is coming here to make dinner for us and if you try anything, as God as my witness, you'll be sorry," he threatened. "Now, go upstairs and get yourself together," he ordered. At first Annabelle didn't move. "Do you think I'm playing games with you?" he growled so loud, Annabelle took off and raced up the stairs. She ran into the room and shut the door and remembered it was no way she could lock him out because it had a keyless lock on the door. She began to search the room for a phone, but there wasn't one. She ran over to the window and looked out and there wasn't a soul in sight.

"Oh, my God, what am I going to do?" she cried in a panic and after a few moments of searching the drawers and closet for at least a weapon, she came up with nothing. She stopped and just caught her breath. Her mind was racing, and she didn't have a clue how she was going to get away from him, so she slid down he wall, onto the floor and then sobbed in her hands.

Jamal had second thoughts about what he had planned, and he wished he would have just taken her to Daisy Mae's, but she belonged to him and he had to find a way to fix it. He didn't want everyone to know that he had somehow ruined another member of his brother's church and he definitely did not need everyone hating him, because of Annabelle. Everyone adored her, so he just had to win her back over or at least convince her to keep her mouth shut. He knew he couldn't keep her there forever, but he planned to keep her there long enough for them to settle their differences. Hell, he'd be willing to pay her fifty thousand cash to keep her mouth closed about the situation and hopefully that would be it and afterwards he'd deal with Kat's conniving self. He hated himself for what he had done to Annabelle, because he truly loved her, but what he'd done and said was irreversible and he had a strong feeling that Annabelle would never forgive him. He went up to check on Annabelle and when she looked up at him, he reached out his hand. She didn't take it. "Listen, don't make this hard, Annabelle. You know I'm not all bad."

"I thought that, but I see I was sadly wrong," she said in a low whisper and dropped her head feeling defeated yet again.

"I know what you may think of me now, but I love you and as a woman of God I need you to forgive and give me another chance."

"I can forgive you, Jamal, but I will not give you another chance," she said.

"Let me help you up, Belle, please stop being difficult," he said with his arm still extended. She didn't dare touch him. "You see what you do? You make me talk to you and treat you like I do, because you act like you can't just go with the flow, now give me your damn hand," he yelled, and she then put her hand in his. He pulled her up from the floor and pulled her into his arms and put a kiss on her lips but she tried to pull away.

"The more you fight me on this, it's going to make matters worse, so I suggest you let me have it my way, Belle."

Her eyes welled and then she stopped resisting. He kissed her, and she kissed him back.

"See how easy that was. Now please stop all of this damn crying and let me make things right with you. Stop being so damn stubborn."

She didn't say anything. Daniel will be here soon and when he gets here, he can't see you looking all broken." She still said nothing. "Do you hear me?" he yelled and held her by her waist tighter.

She nodded. "Yes," she said, and he could tell the way her body shook that she was terrified. Satisfied that she feared him, he knew he'd be able to control the situation, so he said, "Now listen at me real good, I'm not going to hurt you, as long as you just go along with the program. All I want is for us to get back on track. You know I love you, Belle, and if you just say we're okay, we can get back to being happy. Do we have an understanding?" He was looking down his nose at her.

Annabelle stared at Jamal long and hard, and she had had a million and one things going on in her head and none of them were positive. All she could think of was, *Lord why me*? She lowered her head, feeling defeated.

"Did you hear what I said?"

"Yes," she mumbled and then she fell silent again.

He released the hold he had on her waist and she went for the bathroom and locked the door behind her. Then she went to the vanity and looked into the mirror. Her makeup was ruined, and she looked as if she had had a fight, so then she turned on the water.

"God, why did you allow him to do me like this?" she questioned.

Silence at first and then she heard. "I didn't, Pastor James told you not to go that direction and you went anyway."

Annabelle spun around as if the voice came from someone that was there. Then she realized that was the voice of God telling her that she had gotten herself into that mess. "I know I did this, but please God just get me out of this?" she prayed.

The bathroom was still stocked with her make-up, toiletries and smell goods. She cleaned up and when Jamal tapped she knew it was time to go downstairs and pretend they were in bliss. She opened the door and Jamal apparently had used the guest bathroom in one of the other spare rooms to change because he was dressed in black slacks and a button down and doused with one of his expensive Creed colognes.

"I'm almost done dressing," she said, going for her suitcase.

"Daniel is already preparing dinner, so don't be long," he said and leaned in to kiss her. "Now I'm going to warn you, Belle, don't try no slick mess, because I pay my employees well to mind their business and Daniel knows to mind his own business."

With that, she nodded and made a mental note to not act a fool. For all she knew, Daniel could be in on it just like Kat was, so she took heed to Jamal's words.

"I won't try anything crazy, Jamal; I promise."

"That's my girl," he smiled. He kissed her one more time and then he left the room. She went into her suitcase and willed herself not to let a tear fall. She'd just have to play nice and do whatever he wanted her to do until she could come up with a plan to get the hell away from that demon.

Later after dinner, Annabelle was upstairs in the tub and Jamal was in the living room wondering how things will pan out with him and Annabelle. He wanted so bad for her to say she'd stay with him because losing her was going to hurt him. His phone buzzed in his pocket. He went for it and swiped the screen. It was James.

-HAVE YOU SEEN OR HEARD FROM ANNABELLE

-NAH, NOT SINCE SHE WENT TO SEE A FRIEND OF HERS AT THE SHELTER

- I'VE BEEN CALLING HER & AND IT'S GOIN STRAIGHT 2 VOICEMAIL

-BRAH I'M IN THE MIDDLE OF SOMETHING RIGHT NOW. I'LL GET A HOLD OF HER & LET HER KNOW TO HIT U BCK

-THANKS

With that, Jamal turned off his phone. He then tossed it to the side and then stood and headed up stairs. Annabelle was relaxing in the tub, so he let the lid down and sat.

"I swear to you, I'm sorry for all this."

"I accept your apology, Jamal. Honestly, I do, but I just wanna leave."

"I know, but I want us to be together, Belle. I don't want to lose you over this. I didn't know she recorded us."

"Alright fine, I will do whatever you want, and I won't say a word about this to anyone and I will give you another chance, just take me back."

He eyed her down, because that was just too sudden, so he said, "Okay, we'll go back tomorrow." He stood and leaned in and kissed the top of her head and went back downstairs. He'd decided he'd see how the next day went. If Annabelle was serious, he'd watch her behavior and then and only then, he'd take her back.

The following morning, Jamal was up bright and early. He was downstairs in the kitchen fixing some hot coffee. He was tired and hadn't had too much sleep at all because he held on to Annabelle tight that night to make sure she didn't try any funny business. He had locked all the doors with the door stoppers on the top and bottom, so if she tried the doors, she'd need a chair to reach the top ones, making her attempt to escape more difficult. There weren't many windows that opened and if she were to open one the security alarm would alert him, so he hoped she didn't try to make an escape.

He sipped his coffee from a plastic cup that had a green and white Starbucks logo on it. Then he poured Annabelle a cup and took it upstairs to her. She was still sleeping in the bed. He didn't know if he should wake her up or leave her sleep at this point. He sat her cup of coffee down on the night stand. Then he paused for a brief moment and took himself another sip from his cup. He walked over and hit the button for the curtains and they parted, letting the morning sunlight shine into the bedroom. It was so bright, he squinted, but he didn't close the curtains.

"Close the curtain back, please," Annabelle whispered from the bed.

Jamal turned around and faced her, then he moved over towards the bed. She was lying on her back with the covers pulled up to her neck and her eyes were closed.

"Are you about to get up?" Jamal asked.

Her eyes were still closed. "Are we about to head back?" she asked him.

"There is no rush for us to get back, Annabelle. Since we're out here we can take a little time to enjoy our day."

Annabelle didn't respond, she just turned her back to him. Jamal shrugged his shoulders and turned back around and faced the window and continued to sip his coffee. His eyes looked out over the mountain top, the scene was breathtaking and for a moment he'd thought about the entire situation with him and Annabelle. *What am I doing?* He asked himself. This is definitely not who I want to be anymore. He shook his head, reached inside his pocket and pulled out two Xanax pills. He popped them in his mouth and sipped the coffee again to wash them down his throat. Jamal was lost in thought again, staring far out into the wilderness. But it was like he was looking at nothing but an empty space. Before he knew it five minutes had passed by.

Ten minutes.

Fifteen minutes. He took a deep breath and turned around and walked towards the bed, he sat his coffee cup down on the night stand and sat down on the bed and removed his slippers. The pills were already taking its effect and he felt like a tire with a slow leak. He finally laid down in the bed next to Annabelle and moved over closer to her. She was laying on her right side with her back to him. He inched his lips to the side of her neck and kissed her. Her body didn't tense, and he had a sense of relief, that maybe they would be okay.

Jamal's eyes were slowly closing, because the Xanax pills were creeping on him fast. He turned his lips into a smile and then he reached up and touched the side of her arm.

"I'm so sorry, Belle," he whispered and then he drifted off to sleep. Annabelle laid there motionless and listened to him breathe. She would wait for at least another fifteen minutes before she would try to ease up out of the bed. Nervousness had washed over her entire body, and she could feel the small beads of sweat forming on her forehead. But that wasn't enough to change her mind of making her escape. She tried to control her breathing to the point that she was nearly holding her breath.

Jamal's snores began to thunder so she inched away, but when he moved, she froze. His snores grew louder, so she knew he was out cold.

Minutes passed, and her heart thumbed so hard inside of her chest that she thought that he could probably hear it. Annabelle took a deep breath, and she moved away from him, and she was praising God that he didn't budge.

The edge of the bed were a few inches away, but she took a couple tiny inches at a time. Her adrenaline was on high and when she reached the edge of the bed, she slid down to the floor and got on all fours. She rose up a little and looked back at Jamal again, and he was still snoring like a bear. She imagined he'd wake himself with how loud he was, but she just hoped to make it out the door before he regained consciousness. She crawled away from the bed, moving silently and swiftly until she got to the door. She reached up and twisted the knob, pulled the door open just enough so she could get through it. Annabelle slipped out in the hallway and quietly closed the door behind her. She hurried down the stairs and she scrambled looking for the keys to the SUV, but she couldn't find them. She quickly looked for his cellphone, but neither was in plain sight. She begged God for strength and prayed that the keys and phone were not upstairs, because going back up wouldn't be smart. She then remembered all of her shoes were upstairs, so she had to find those keys to keep from running barefoot in the woods, plus she knew she'd get lost out there.

She paused. "Okay, think Annabelle, think," she whispered. "God be my rock!" she prayed and looked at the door and then looked back up at the stairs. She knew it was risky, but she eased back up and softly opened the door. Jamal's snores were still blasting in the room and she tried to keep as quiet as she could. She trembled uncontrollably as she eased her jeans and sweatshirt from the top of the chair. She grabbed her shoes and looked around to see if she could spot his phone or keys and she came up short on both. Jamal's body shifted, and she stood still, silently begging God to not let him wake up and he didn't.

She eased out the door and made it back to the lower level. She hurried and dressed and then she just decided to run. It was early in the a.m., so she had enough daylight to at least make it to the main road. She tried the front door first and then she realized that there were door stoppers and the top one was impossible for her to reach. She began to panic and knew she had to get out of there, so she went to the kitchen and went to the window. She unlocked it and as soon as she lifted it, it stopped at an inch and the alarm blared. She thought she would faint because even when she shut it, it still wouldn't stop, and she knew he'd be coming for her. She ran to the counter and snatched a knife from the set and then grabbed a chair. She raced to the front door, stood on it and then her body was knocked off the chair and then the knife slid away from her.

"Where you think you going?" he roared.

Annabelle turned over to face him, she was scared for her life. He tried to grab her, but she kicked her feet wildly and landed a good one in the center of his face and he fell back. She was so desperate to get out of there and scooted back and she felt around for the knife like a crazy person.

"Annabelle, what in the hell is wrong with you?" Jamal yelled over the blaring alarm. He moved towards her again and finally grabbed her. His right arm went way back down to South Florida, came up through Savannah, Georgia and around Aiken, South Carolina then back to Atlanta, and by the time his balled fist connected with the left side of her jaw, her neck snapped hard to the right, spit flung from her mouth and in slow motion, she fell. Annabelle screamed and then her right hand finally landed on the knife. She held it up. "Jamal, stay back," she cried.

"Belle, give me that damn knife, now!" he growled.

She shook. "Please, stay back. I just want to leave, that's all. Just let me leave," she pleaded, but the look in his eyes said he wasn't going to let her leave. She asked God for strength because her fear was replaced by survival and Annabelle plunged the knife in his inner thigh and he wailed out "Stupppiiddd motha...!" He tried to reach out for her, but he fell over. Annabelle tossed the knife and ran back to the door. She got the turned over chair and put it back to the door and got on it and undid the latch. She got down and when she snatched the door open. Standing before her stood a uniformed officer.

"Ma'am, we got the alarm signal. Is everything al 'right?" he asked.

She shook her head and then Jamal yelled out," Call an ambulance, she tried to kill me. The officer rushed by Annabelle and Annabelle went and sat on the wooden bench. It was over, and she just put her hands up to her face and sobbed.

"Officer, thank God you're here," Jamal cried. Although he pressed on his wound, the blood was pouring out. Immediately the officer called for an ambulance and went to assist Jamal. The officer ran into the kitchen and came back with a dish towel.

"Mr. Wright, tell me what happened?" the officer questioned.

Jamal took short deep breaths because he could feel himself getting weak. "That's my lady. She and I were having problems and I told her once we get back to Atlanta, we needed to go our separate ways and she got angry and we exchanged words, next thing I know, she pulls out a knife on me. I tried to retrieve the knife, but she tried to fight me. We tussled, and then she stabbed me," Jamal lied, and the officer nodded.

"Just relax, Mr. Wright; help is on the way," he said.

Jamal nodded, but he could feel himself fading and he felt as if he was going to pass out. "Sit tight, we got you," he heard and then he blacked out.

12

---

amal seemed to be slipping into the twilight zone. He could see the lake outside and the beautiful mountains far beyond it, and there were canoes out there. Three of them to be exact, across the water it looked as if diamonds were strewn out across it. When he began to float, he instantly knew that it may have been the Xanax, Adderall or the heroin that he was addicted to that had him feeling like that. A light breeze was rushing across his face, he looked down at his leg, the bleeding had stopped and there was no scar, or trace of the incident. The euphoric feeling that he was experiencing was unexplainable.

"Get up, Jamal," he imagined he heard and he opened his eyes to her angelic face. He reached out to touch her, but his hand went right through her and she smiled at him. He could feel his body rocking side to side and he then saw Annabelle driving them in the clouds. He blinked again and then they were back at the lake. He could hear the creatures of the night making their usual sounds, but when he reached to touch Annabelle, he could not grab her.

Then he saw himself at ten years old playing in the front yard with his older brother, James. They both had had on leather baseball gloves *and were playing catch together, they were wearing cut off denim jeans, matching Braves jerseys and Stan Smith Adidas.*

"Catch the ball this time," James yelled to him.

"Just throw it."

James tossed the baseball, but it never came down. Jamal was looking up in the sky for it to come down, but it never did. The clouds were white and pretty, so he leaped into the air to get it, but he couldn't catch it. Then the sounds around him became real. He could hear the doctor giving commands and he could feel them poking and prying and pulling, but he couldn't open his eyes. He tried so hard, but then his efforts were halted when his heart stopped, and he took his last breath.

Annabelle hopped out of the police car and rushed inside of the hospital. They had already rolled Jamal to the back and she looked around for someone to give her an update, but no one was at the front counter. The hospital was so small that it resembled a clinic in size and Annabelle wondered if they'd have to air lift Jamal to the city. She paced back and forth and then finally a mid-aged brown skin stout woman walked out of the double doors.

"Ma'am, ma'am," Annabelle said in a panic. "They just brought my boyfriend, I mean Jamal Wright in in an ambulance."

"Ma'am, they are working on him now. I suggest you call your family because it's not looking too good. He's lost a significant amount of blood."

Annabelle shook her head. "I don't have my phone. It's broken, and I don't know who to call first."

"Well, have a seat for now until the doctors can speak with you."

She nodded and headed for the waiting area. She then saw the officers come in and they stopped at the nurses' station and then she allowed them to go back. Annabelle's nerves were all over the place and she shook uncontrollably. An hour later, the doctor finally came out to talk to her.

"Mrs. Wright?" he said.

"No, I'm Annabelle Humphrey, Jamal is... I mean, was my boyfriend."

"I'm sorry, but we did all we could," he said.

Annabelle could not believe her eyes. "What do you mean, doc?" she questioned.

"Mr. Wright didn't make it," he clarified.

"Noooooo," Annabelle wailed. She never wanted him dead. She kept shaking her head and her eyes were shut tight. Her head jerked back, and her eyes shot open when she felt someone pull her back by the arm.

"Annabelle Humphrey, you are under arrest for the murder of Jamal Wright." Annabelle heard those words and then she fainted.

❧

WHEN ANNABELLE OPENED HER EYES, SHE WAS HANDCUFFED TO A gurney. She looked around to find herself behind a curtain. Her mouth was dry, and she wondered if she had dreamed everything, but when she looked down and saw the specks of Jamal's blood on her clothes and felt the pains from her face and body, she knew that it was all real. "Hello," she yelled out, and within seconds the curtain was snatched back.

"Miss Humphrey, how are you feelin?" the doctor asked before shining a light in her face. He checked both her eyes and then stuck the light back into his white coat pocket.

"Tired and I could use some water. My face is sore," she said. Her voice was low and raspy.

"I'll have the nurse to bring you some water. We got X-rays of you, but I must warn you, they are about to take you in."

"For what, I didn't murder Jamal," she defended and then the officer, appeared behind the doctor. Her heart raced. "Listen, this is all a misunderstanding," she pleaded, but the officer just read her rights to her. He uncuffed her, and she moved to

the end of edge of the bed, the tears began to run down her cheeks.

"Please stand," the officer said, and she obliged. She didn't get her water, she was escorted out to the police car and then put into the back. When they got to the station, they put her in a room and she just sat there for what seemed like an eternity. She sat at an old worn down wooden desk and then a tall white detective with cold blue eyes, thin lips and huge hands walked in and sat across from her. He was dressed in jeans, cowboy boots, a white button up shirt and brown cowboy hat. "So, let's start from the beginning and I want the truth," he said. His tone was stern and serious, and Annabelle was prepared to tell him everything.

"Where do I start?" she quizzed.

"Let's start with this morning," he suggested.

"I'd like to, but I need to start a little further back, so you'd understand."

"Okay, I'm listening," he said.

Annabelle, let out a sigh, and then began at the day they met, two hours later her cuffs were off, and they allowed her a cup of coffee. They left her alone and Annabelle's hands trembled so much, she could barely drink her bitter coffee.

Finally, when he returned, he had a female officer with him. She was short and stout with gray hair that was pulled back in a ponytail. "Please stand up for me, Miss Humphrey?"

Annabelle was confused. She had told them everything. Why wasn't they letting her go home. "Why? I'm innocent. Why can't I go?" she cried.

The detective smiled, showing his brown stained teeth and said "Honey, you're still under arrest. We got your little statement, which don't 'mount to a hill of beans, so until you can go before the judge tomorrow, you'll be right here with us tonight."

"You can't be serious," she objected.

"Dead serious, just like your boyfriend that you killed," he spat.

Annabelle shook her head but allowed the lady officer to take her to another room. She was handed an orange jumpsuit and some dingy panties. Some socks and a toothbrush and toothpaste; it was all stuffed inside gray plastic bin. Annabelle looked at the officer.

"Is it okay for me to make a phone call?"

"You can make one before I take you to your cell," she said, "But first, you got to strip and change into the orange," she folded her arms across her chest and leaned up against the wall and studied Annabelle for a second. She said, "I'm not sure if you know or not, but it hasn't been a murder in this town in well over ten years. So, don't expect them to go easy on you. Plus, you're brown, so if you do have a relationship with God the way you said back there in interrogation, I suggest you start praying, because they'd love to have this kind of publicity here."

"I'm not a murderer, officer. I'm a child of God that just got caught up in a situation. Just watch, I'll be going home very soon."

"Well, that's definitely the spirit to have. Do you have any family here in this town?"

"Only God, he's all the family that I need," Annabelle said, feeling defeated. Other than Daisy Mae and her church family, she had no one and she knew God would be the only one to save her from that entire situation.

The officer laughed at her statement and said, "I hear you, missy." Then her smiled faded just as fast as it appeared. She opened the door with her back and stood there and propped it open for Annabelle to walk through.

Annabelle stepped out after she was in the orange jump suit and she then handed the paper bag with her clothes in it to the lady officer.

"These are now going in as evidence, so you most likely won't see these items again unless you go to trial."

She nodded. The woman led the way to three holding cells

and only one cell had a woman in there, lying on the bed with her back to them facing the wall. The woman opened the cell next to that one and Annabelle walked in. She had never been to jail in her life, and she was grateful she was in that tiny town and there weren't any hardcore criminals there to taunt her. She had to think and trying to play tough was the last thing she needed right now.

"Ummm, my phone call," Annabelle reminded the officer.

"I'll be back after I go and log in this evidence," she said holding up the bag with Annabelle's blood-stained clothes. Annabelle just grabbed the bars and watched her walk away. She then rushed over to the bed, went onto her knees and started crying out to God. After praying, she sat on the lumpy bed and started thinking about the big picture. What will the church members say? What will Pastor James say? Everything was all bad and she needed God more than she needed anything if she was going to walk free.

13

*I*t was a little after three in the morning when Pastor James' phone rung and woke him up out of his sleep. In the darkness, he reached over on the nightstand and grabbed his cellphone. The name displayed across the screen read: Mom. He frowned and wiped the sleep out of his eyes and then answered the phone.

"Hey mama."

"James, wake up, something happened to Jamal," she cried.

James tried to understand why his mother was crying into the phone. He snatched the covers away from his body and stood up from the bed.

"What...What are you talking about?" he asked. It was late, and he was confused, so he urged his mother to calm down and tell him what was going on.

She took a deep breath and then sighed, "Lawd, ham mercy, they say my baby gone," she sobbed.

James rubbed his hand over his face and asked, "Who told you this mama? Who are they?" he asked. "Where did they call from and did you get a number?"

His mother went on and on for the next few minutes, as she

cried uncontrollably. Still he could barely understand what she was saying, and he was glad she finally got around to reciting the number. When he hung up with her, he called the number that she had given him. He was finally wide awake, and the bedroom light was on. James paced as the phone rang and then it went to voicemail. 'Thanks for calling Detective Brady Young, leave your name and number and I'll get right back at you."

Beep!

"Yes, my name is James Wright and my mother just gave me your number. I'm calling in concerns of my brother, Jamal Wright. Can you please call me as soon as possible," he said and then hit end. He then tried Annabelle, because she'd have to know something, and her line went straight to voicemail. Not understanding the news he had received, he dialed Jamal's number and it rang, but it too went to voicemail. He walked into the bathroom and flipped on the light and looked at himself in the mirror. He sat his phone down on the granite vanity and then began to pray. "Dear heavenly Father, please let my little brother be alright." His phone rung as soon as he was saying that. He looked down at it and saw the same number that he'd just called, and he answered right away, "Hello."

"Mr. Wright, I'm Detective Young. Sorry I missed your call and I know you called about your brother, Jamal Wright?"

"Yes, I did. My mother said that you spoke to her and informed her that my brother had passed?" James asked hoping that the information was false.

"I'm so sorry for your loss. He was pronounced dead this morning at a little after nine o'clock."

"And it took you this long to contact us?"

"I know, but it took a long time to gather evidence from the crime scene and to get your brother's id, and contact information. I'm sorry, Mr. Wright, it's a process."

"Evidence, what evidence? I don't follow."

"Mr. Wright, your brother was murdered. He was stabbed by his girlfriend," he said, and James almost dropped the phone.

"I'm sorry, but that has to be some kind of mistake. Annabelle would never do anything to hurt anyone, especially not Jamal, she loves him."

"Well, you can come to the station in the morning. She will be going before the judge. She didn't ask for a lawyer and since this is such a huge crime, I don't know if she'll be awarded bail. Your brother gave a statement to one of our officers before he went unconscious, so things aren't looking too good for her. She claims it was self-defense, but we got your brother's statement before he died, and we believe otherwise," he added. After that, Pastor James didn't hear anything else that the detective was saying. He just stood, dropped his phone, and then he fell to the floor on his knees and opened his mouth, but no sounds came out. The tears he tried to hold back began to stream down his cheeks. Then the scream came from his mouth so loud that it sounded like a wounded animal. "My Goooooooddddddd, what happened?" he sobbed. His heart was crushed, and it felt as if he was losing his breath. Tears fell from his face and rolled down his neck and began soaking his pajama shirt. Just then, he clasped his fingers together and started praying through his tears. His body was jerking and hiccupping and moments later, he just fell on the middle of the bathroom floor and allowed the tears to flow.

By six o'clock, he was showered and dressed. He walked outside and got into a Lexus LS 500 and pressed the push start button. When he pulled out the driveway, he headed to his mother's house. She lived in Fayetteville, Georgia and the drive from where he lived would probably take forty minutes to get there. Pastor James was trying to picture in his mind what could have happened with Annabelle and his brother, but he couldn't figure out what could have possibly gone wrong to lead to his brother's death. His hands gripped the steering wheel tighter and he took a deep breath to calm himself. But at that point, it wasn't happening. His palms were beginning to sweat as he weaved through traffic. His mind went back to the early nineties when he and his brother went to one of the Atlanta Falcons home games at the Georgia dome.

They both wanted to see Deion Sanders play in person. When they got their seats, James told his younger brother, "I want to see you out there on the football field just like this."

"I'm definitely going to be a superstar one day. I just don't know if I'll be a football superstar. But what I do know is that I'm going to make Mama proud and get her out that raggedy house in the swats."

"Yeah, that's the goal, and that's something that we're going to work on together. Two places I'm not trying to visit you at, in prison or your gravesite. I'm older than you. So that means you need to live longer than me. And I'm saying that to say this, don't let the streets be an option."

"Oh, most definitely not. The only weakness that I have is these beautiful women."

James snapped out of his thoughts and put his focus back on the road. A moment later, his cellphone rung through the car speakers. He answered it from the button on the steering wheel. "Hello."

"Pastor James," a soft kind voice said from the other end.

"Sister Daisy, Good morning." He already recognized her voice.

"I'm sure you heard about your brother and I'm really sorry. Annabelle just called me collect from the county jail and said she tried calling me yesterday, but I wasn't home. "I just don't know what to do," she cried.

Pastor James was staring straight ahead but he was listening at Daisy Mae, her words had had him feeling down for a second. His eyes cut to the rearview mirror, the early morning traffic was getting thick and that made him slow down a little.

"Well, as of now, let's just pray over the situation. I'm heading over to my mother's house now and then we're going up to find out what really happened. What else did Annabelle tell you?"

"Nothing much, she didn't have long. She insists that she needs to talk to you. She said she doesn't have her cellphone, so she didn't have your number to call you. She just happened to remember mine by heart," Daisy Mae explained sadly.

That made Pastor James swallow hard. He didn't know what to say at that moment, negative thoughts were going through his mind. According to the detective, she had murdered his brother and she wanted to talk to him. Then he spoke into the car speakers. "I can't speak with her now, not until I know what's going on, Daisy Mae," he said and then ended the call. He knew Daisy Mae would be on Annabelle's side and until he got more details, Annabelle was the last person he wanted to feel sympathy for.

14

*A*nnabelle was a nervous wreck. Hours had passed since she'd spoken with Sister Daisy Mae over the phone. That was the only person's number that she had to call collect. The only friend that she could rely on. She didn't have her cell, so she didn't remember anyone's number other than Jamal's and Daisy Mae's. She stood with her back up against the wall right next to the pay phone. Annabelle needed to talk with somebody because she didn't know anything about anything when it came to being in jail and she was supposed to go before the judge sometime that day. She didn't have a lawyer, so she had no clue what to do. The only thing she did knew was that she wasn't supposed to be there. She tried to get herself together, because she was frustrated and on top of that, mourning Jamal.

Every time she thought about him actually being dead, she sobbed her eyes out. She couldn't even sleep the night before, because of how hurt she was that he was gone, and it was because of her. She wished she'd done things differently and wished she could just go back, but that was impossible. She knew God wasn't pleased, but she also believed that he had forgiven her because she didn't intend to end his life. She was no murderer and would never harm anyone on purpose.

She just hoped she posted bail, so she could try and find a good attorney. She had access to an account with over one hundred grand and if she made bail, she could get herself a good lawyer. She tried to remember her aunt's number, but she came up blank.

A moment later, the female officer that was there the night before approached her.

"Look, you have a visitor and then you go before the judge at three," she said.

Annabelle nodded and followed the woman. When she led her to a small room, Annabelle was so happy to see Daisy Mae and she ran and hugged her tight.

"Thank you so much for coming. I am so happy to see you."

"You knew I would. I got my grandson to bring me and I talked to Pastor James, but he needs a little time," she said.

She nodded. "I understand. Let's sit," she said.

"Only ten minutes," the officer said and both Annabelle and Daisy Mae looked at her.

"Yes, ma'am," Annabelle said.

"Listen, how are you child? What happened?"

"Sister Daisy, it was an accident," Annabelle cried. She got emotional and had to take a deep breath. "I can't go into much detail, but Jamal turned into the devil on me and all that wooing he had done to make me fall for him was just a trap," she said.

"What did he do to you?"

"He did something so foul that I don't even want to repeat it. Well, when I asked him to take me back to your place he pretended he would, but he had put something in my tea and when I woke up I was at the lake house and he refused to let me leave. He broke my phone and I tried to leave and he caught me and that's when I... when I...." she cried.

"No, no, Annabelle, you don't have to say no more."

"They wanna prosecute me for murder," she cried, nearly breaking down.

"Well, when do you see the judge?" Daisy Mae asked her, she was hurting so much for Annabelle that she was nearly in tears also.

"This afternoon," she said.

"Well, I'm going to stay and even if I have to put up my house for your bail, I'm not going to leave you here alone," Daisy Mae said.

A smile graced Annabelle's face and she squeezed Daisy Mae's hands.

"Thank you so much, Daisy Mae. I have some money in an account that Jamal had set up for me and access to another account that we are joint on. The account in my name should have at least twenty to thirty grand in it. It was just for essentials and if I wanted to shop; maybe that will help."

"It should, let's just see what the judge says," Daisy Mae suggested. Annabelle breathed a sigh of relief. "Let's pray before our time is up."

"Yes, ma'am," she said.

They bowed their heads and Daisy Mae prayed, asking God to forgive them first and foremost for their sins and to be with them during that difficult time. She asked God for strength and courage and for peace. Before she said amen, she also prayed for Jamal and she prayed that his soul was resting in heaven. "Amen," she said.

Annabelle looked at her curiously. "Daisy Mae, I know I'm not as mature as you are in Christ, but after the horrible things that Jamal had done to me, what makes you think he's with the Father in heaven now?"

Daisy Mae giggled a bit. "Well, Annabelle, the old saying is it's never too late to repent. Only God can decide who is thrown in hell or received in heaven, so we don't know his last words, or if he had a contrite heart when he spoke his last words, so we can never say where a soul ends up."

Annabelle didn't truly understand, but she nodded. She opened her mouth to speak, but the female's voice blared, "Times up."

She rolled her eyes and then stood.

"I have to go, but you will be here when I go before the judge at three, right?"

"Yes, I'll just go have a bite to eat and come back."

With that, Annabelle followed the officer back to her holding cell.

"You do know that this judge is as tough as they come and outside of these walls there have been reporters and cameras flashing, so your chances of walking are slim to zero," she informed Annabelle.

Her hands began to shake. "You can't be serious, right? I mean, I'm no criminal, and I've never broken the law in my life," Annabelle protested.

"Well, this town doesn't get much more than traffic tickets or old man Wilson getting drunk and exposing himself. Now, if your bail is denied, you will be transferred until your trial date and it's nothing like county jail."

"Is county jail worse?" Annabelle questioned.

"Worse than here, but not worse than prison."

The word prison rang in Annabelle's ears. "I'm innocent. I didn't do anything to be sent to prison," she cried.

"Well, if you go to trial that will be for a judge or jury to decide. However, for now you need to worry about making bail."

Annabelle just nodded and walked into her cell. She had no idea what time it was, but she was grateful that she had time to pray. She prayed until she dozed off to sleep. The sounds of the keys unlocking her cell woke her and she quickly sat up.

"It's that time," the female officer said.

Annabelle stood to her feet and wiped the crust from the

corners of her eyes and then walked towards the guard, but she stopped her and handcuffed her.

"Is this necessary?" she asked.

"What do you think," she said, and it was like Annabelle had noticed her nametag for the first time. He name was L. Hughes and Annabelle tried to guess what her name was as she was escorted to a room that was smaller than a classroom. It had a judge's bench, a seat where she assumed people testified to the right, but it only had two rows of four chairs. She was happy to see Daisy Mae sitting in one of the chairs as promised. There were the arresting officers, she assumed the prosecuting attorney, because she was pushed to the table with a man that looked like he was trying to get organized.

"Sit here," Officer Hughes said, and she took a seat next to the middle aged white man who was balding. She wondered if it was stress of the job or hereditary. She sat, and he introduced himself.

"I'm Stanley Bowers and I'm your appointed attorney. I just got your file thirty minutes ago, so I suggest a plea of guilty."

Annabelle's eyes bulged. "I suggest you let me represent myself because there is no way on God's green earth will I plead guilty."

"Listen Miss," he said.

She cut him off., "Annabelle."

"Listen Annabelle, this is like an airtight case with Jamal's statement," he said.

She cut him off again. "Jamal's statement, what statement are you talking about?" She was out on the porch and didn't know that Jamal had said anything, let alone gave a statement.

"Listen Annabelle, this is the deal. You may not get bail and if you plead guilty, we can shoot for a lesser charge."

Annabelle looked up and closed her eyes. "Your will, Lord; not mine, Lord," she said and turned back to her appointed attorney. "Not guilty," she said again.

He let out a breath and then said, "It's your life." They talked about a couple more details before the judge finally took a seat on the bench. The necessary speech was given to bring the court to order and then the judge took over. "Annabelle Humphrey," he said not even looking up at her.

She stood. "Yes, sir," she said barely audible. She was trembling at that point.

"Speak up, Miss Humphrey," he belted.

"Ummm, yes sir," she said.

He read off a bunch of laws, code numbers and proper terms to inform Annabelle of the charges that were being brought up against her. After he took almost four minutes to explain that she was basically being charged for murder in the first degree, he paused and asked. "Annabelle Humphrey, do you understand these charges that have been brought against you."

She nodded as one tear ran down her cheek. "Yes sir, I do," she whimpered.

"How do you plead?" he asked.

"Not guilty your honor and my client has, no priors, never had a run in with the law, and she is an upstanding citizen. She is the Sunday school teacher at her local church and before the tragic incident with Mr. Wright, Miss Humphreys hasn't even had a traffic ticket."

"And the courts are not concerned about the things that Miss Humphrey may or may not have did before the life of an innocent man was taken by her hands counselor and I know where you are going, so don't even attempt to ask, because bail is denied."

"But your honor, it is her right," he countered.

The judge finally looked in their direction.

"Okay, since you got time to waste and feel like hearing your own voice, go ahead."

"Your honor, my client request bail to be set at..." he tried to say.

"Denied," the judge said, cutting him off. "Miss Humphrey

will be transferred tomorrow to the Gilmer County jail, where she will remain until her trial date is set." With that said, he banged his gavel and Annabelle didn't hear anything else. She stood there frozen and it felt like cotton balls were stuffed in her eyes. She just felt her head drop and she didn't snap back to the room until the constant tugging of her arm jerked her back to reality.

"What... what... whaaaattttt just happened?" she asked the attorney and he just shook his head.

"Annabelle, don't worry, honey. I will be there to see you tomorrow as soon as I can," she heard Daisy Mae say, but Officer Hughes was damn near dragging her back to her cell. Her knees were weak and as soon as she removed her handcuffs and slammed the bars behind Annabelle, she fell onto her knees and cried harder than she had ever cried in her life.

The next day, as the judge stated, she was transported. After a cold shower and a change of jumpsuit, she was taken to her new temporary home. She was in a daze and thanked God that even though all eyes were on her, no one said anything to her. She walked in and the Hispanic woman just gave her a nod. She nodded back before she climbed onto the free bed in the cell. Annabelle laid down and turned her back to face the wall, thanking God she didn't say anything to her. This place was definitely different from where she came from. It was loud, and she silently prayed that her arraignment came quick. When she was awakened with a shake, she learned that it was chow time, so she just followed suit.

Once she was seated, a woman across from her spoke. "You don't have to be shy. We ain't gon bite," she said.

"I'm not shy, I just got so much on my mind."

"Like what?" another young lady said and then bit into the sandwich she had in her hands.

"Everything, I mean I never knew I'd end up in prison," she said, and all the ladies burst into laughter.

"Honey, this is county lock up. This ain't prison," one Latina woman said.

"Yes, you have to be convicted of some serious stuff to be in prison."

Annabelle just chewed her dry sandwich and didn't reveal to the ladies that her charges were as serious as they came, she just ate and made small talk. Later, she was able to call Daisy Mae and she told Daisy May about the account and to try to get her a lawyer and she promised she'd try to go by the court and get the right documents for Annabelle to sign for her to have access to her account. Two days later, Annabelle was just trying to stay positive and focused.

Her eyes locked in on an older looking black woman that was walking out of her cell, she was holding a folded newspaper under her arm and was holding a cup of coffee in the other hand. When Annabelle saw her sit down at one of the stainless-steel tables by herself, she walked right over to her. "Excuse me, can I talk to you for a second?" she asked her.

The dark-skinned sister, with a natural afro with a few sprinkles of gray in it looked up at Annabelle. "Sure, go right ahead."

Annabelle sat down across from her and placed her elbows on the table. Then she extended her hand. "I'm Annabelle."

The lady shook Annabelle's hand and said, "I already know who you are," she said with a country accent. "My name is Tina."

Annabelle's eyebrows bunched together in confusion. "How do you know me?" she asked.

"A murder charge is big news and those guards tell your story for you, baby. And even if you ain't told a soul up in here, trust me, they know." Annabelle's eyes went down to the table then they went back up to Tina. She was thinking to herself and shaking her head at the same time. When she took a deep breath, she said, "I just don't know what to say or do at this point."

Tina sipped her coffee and sat it back down. "Do you have a lawyer?" she asked her.

"Not, not yet. But, my sister in Christ Daisy Mae, well she's more like my mom, is going to work on that for me," Annabelle said. "Won't they give me one?"

Tina laughed. "I see you really green to all of this. Listen at me real good, don't take this situation lightly sweetheart. You killed a man and you sitting up here acting like you locked up for writing bad checks or something. A murder charge can get you a life sentence, you'll probably have to do thirty years just off of that. Now on the flip side and this all depends on the case and the evidence that they got against you, they may offer you a plea for manslaughter. If I'm not mistaken, voluntary manslaughter can range from one to ten years, but don't quote me on that. But I do know that involuntary manslaughter has a max of ten years. If they offer you a plea, take it. Now, you may have to do a few years or may get probation. Or you might beat the whole case. Either or, it's better than getting that life sentence for murder."

"I already pleaded not guilty," Annabelle said.

"That don't matter. Once you lawyer up, you can change your plea."

Annabelle sat quiet for a long moment, thinking about changing her plea. A life sentence for something she didn't mean to do was just too much. No way could she live the rest of her life behind bars. I'm not even going to prison. Annabelle rubbed her hand over her face and then looked up towards the ceiling.

"Look, don't panic, wait until your friend gets you that lawyer and then decide."

"How much will a good one cost?"

"A good one? Probably about twenty thousand or more," Tina said and sipped from her coffee again with her eyes locked on Annabelle.

"Twenty thousand dollars is a lot, but I got a little to handle that. I just need to sign some papers for Daisy Mae to get to it," she said, thinking of the money that Jamal had put into an account for her.

"Well, at least you can afford a lawyer, most of us can't afford one. And if you are facing murder charges, the state of Georgia has a couple of judges that don't take it easy on us brown girls. You better pray you don't end up getting Judge Henry. They call him Hang 'em High Henry." She rubbed the back of her hand. "You see the color of our skin, well you are a little lighter than me, but you still black. Don't take these people for a joke, sweetheart. They will hang yo' butt if you go in their courtroom playing."

Annabelle remained quiet again, because she was at a loss for words. She took a deep breath and then another and then another one. Then she asked Tina, "So, what are you locked up for?"

"Just a misdemeanor, I flattened all the tires on my husband's car." She laughed loudly.

"If he wasn't a police officer, I'd be home. But, they arrested me for that dumb crap." She then stood up. "That's my cue to leave," she said. Annabelle turned to see an officer in the booth waving her hands. "My bond had been posted. I'm about to go home now," she said and extended her hand to Annabelle. "You stay safe and stay prayed up, and may God bless you on your journey," she said and then walked through the sally port doors. Annabelle turned around and watched her leave. She then got up and went back to her cell that she shared with another Hispanic woman. Annabelle climbed up on her top bunk and laid flat out on her back and stared at the ceiling. Then she began talking out loud. "God, what happened?" she questioned and then quietly waited to hear an answer. When there was no answer she said, "So, this is how it goes? I was doing good, minding my own business, and I call myself turning my life over to you, Christ, my Lord and Savior. And this is the reward that I get for following the right steps as a Christian?"

No answer.

Annabelle closed her eyes and then she just tried to relax her mind and not focus on her situation. God was not a person so why was she waiting to hear from him as if he was? She just settled and got quiet and then she could hear the spirit of God and she had to blink to make sure she was hearing his voice. All of sudden the Words of God rang in her spirit and she could hear Him say, "Where is your faith? The choices were yours; you put you in this situation with the choices you have made. Yes, your walk started with me on a clean note, but you allowed Satan to take you down a road with him, that you chose to be on, but I am with you and will always be with you as long as you seek me in righteousness. You can't have it both ways. Things of God is of God and I am with you, but things of the world I have no parts. You have to repent and own up to your parts." She heard, and she understood.

It was clear that God was with her, but the choice to be with Jamal and all the things she did with Jamal was hers and hers alone. "Just please Lord, have mercy on me and don't let murder be my punishment," she cried and then meditated on God hoping that he'd continue to speak to her, and the last thing she remembered the spirit say to her before dozing off was, "I am always with you, but you can't waiver or lose faith."

She whispered, "Thank you, Father. Your will will be done." She drifted off into a deep sleep and she dreamt of her mother.

Her mother was lying in her hospital bed, with a shaved head and Annabelle could see that the cancer had taken a toll on her body. Annabelle stood next to her bed and held her hand. It hurt like hell to see her mother laying there helpless. She wished she had had some type of power to heal her, to remove the cancer from her body. "Dear Mama," she began.

Then someone tapped her arm and woke her from her sleep. When Annabelle opened her eyes and turned her head to the side she was looking in the face of the Hispanic woman that she shared the cell with. "Wake up, I need to use the room," she said in her broken English.

Annabelle sat up in her bunk and rubbed her eyes, she saw

that it was two more Hispanic women in the room also. She climbed down from her bunk and walked out the cell without saying a word and when she got out into the open dorm area, she sat at the same table that she was just sitting at a couple of hours before she'd went to sleep. She looked at her cell door and saw that someone from the inside had put a towel up over the door window. Annabelle turned around on the steel seat and walked over to the pay phone. She picked it up and dialed Daisy Mae's number again and waited for her to answer. The phone rung six times and no one picked up from the other end. Annabelle hung it up and dialed it again. She held the phone to her face and turned towards the dorm while she waited for the answer. Then she heard the operator and Daisy Mae say, "yes" on the other end. "Hey baby," Daisy Mae said from the other end.

When Annabelle heard her voice that made her smile. "Well, good evening, Sister Daisy. I got worried for a minute when you didn't answer the first time."

"No baby, listen to me, I don't care what the situation or what anyone think, I'm going to be with you no matter what. Is that understood?"

Annabelle was nodding her head up and down as she talked to her. "Thank you," she whispered. "You don't know how much I appreciate that." Annabelle turned around and faced the wall, she folded her arm and put her face in the crook of it and leaned up against the top of the phone and started sobbing. "I'm not sure what's going on here, Sister Daisy. God said everything will be alright, but why am I going through this?"

"Honestly baby, only God can answer that question and he's the only one that can judge you," she said and then she got quiet for a moment and went on. "I did speak with Pastor James earlier, it's a lot on him. I did tell him that you wanted to speak with him. He didn't really respond because he's in an emotional state right now. This is a heavy blow for all of us, the entire church community."

"I know," Annabelle said and wiped the falling tears from her face with the back of her hand. She was just holding the phone, not knowing what to say to Daisy Mae. "Will you please let everyone at the church know that I'm sorry and that it was all a mistake. I'm sure Pastor James will never forgive me. But sister, I was afraid for my life."

"I know, baby. I'm sure it was something going on that nobody at the church knows about," Daisy Mae said.

Annabelle was now wiping the tears with the collar of her shirt, but she was slowly getting herself together. Listening to Daisy Mae on the other end made her feel way better than she was a few minutes ago. She closed her eyes and took a deep breath. She was desperately trying to get herself together. They were both just holding the phone, waiting for each other to say something, Then Annabelle started to visualize Jamal sitting on the floor bleeding and begging her to call the ambulance. She pressed her lips together. "Sister Daisy, I love you."

"I love you, too, baby."

After that, Annabelle hung up the phone and turned around to many faces. Then she went back to the table and sat down by herself and waited for the ladies to come out of her room. While she waited, she went to sleep at the table and when she woke up, there was an officer standing over her tapping her on her shoulder.

"It's lock down time," she said to Annabelle. She looked the officer in the face and said, "But I haven't took a shower yet."

"You'll have to do that in the morning, we got to count. Go to your cell," she said in a mean and demanding voice.

Annabelle stood up, she looked at her cell before walking to it. Then she looked up at the tall female officer. She had a very untrusting look in her eyes and Annabelle took a mental note of that. Then she looked at her name tag and it read: Crumbly. Annabelle then walked towards the cell and entered. The officer was right on her heels and slammed the door closed behind her.

Her cellmate was laying on her bunk on her back with her hands propped behind her. She said to Annabelle, "You no shower?" She had a smirk on her face.

"She wouldn't let me."

"You wash in sink. Or you won't sleep in here," she said, sat up in her bunk and looked straight at Annabelle.

"What do you mean wash in the sink or I won't sleep in here?" she questioned.

"This is just as much as my room as it is yours." She was getting just a tad bit angry with her attitude. Annabelle was tired and mentally drained, and she was in no mood to deal with foolishness. Annabelle went over and sat on the desk giving her the same stare down.

"Do you believe in, God?"

"Si...si," she answered.

After that, Annabelle talked with her for the next two hours about the Word of God and that changed the entire atmosphere. When Annabelle finally got a chance to lay down, they were calling her name across the intercom letting her know that she had to go to court the next morning.

The next morning when she finally got inside of the courtroom, there was a news camera there. That was all new to her and she was scared out of her mind. She looked around, there was only white faces from the prosecutors table to the court officer and up to the Judge. Hang 'em High Henry was the first thought that came to her mind when she saw the judge. She read the name on the plate and it was definitely him alright. He was looking at her over the top of his wire framed glasses and she looked at him only for a split second. He dropped his head and went back to looking over some paperwork that he had before him. Annabelle was sitting in a leather cushioned chair when she noticed an older looking white man in a tacky gray suit approaching her. He had brown hair and a huge bald spot on the top. He was carrying a briefcase in his left hand and he extended his right hand out to her.

"Good morning. You're Annabelle Humphrey, correct?" he said.

Annabelle shook his hand while nodding her head at the same time.

"Yes, that's me. And you?"

"I'm Attorney Barrett, I was appointed to you to represent you in this case," he said to her. "Now, if you have a paid attorney you don't need me."

"I don't think I have one yet, I didn't think I'd come before the judge this fast?" she asked.

"Have a seat," he said and then he sat. He opened his briefcase in his lap and flipped it open. He quickly removed a notepad and a pen and looked at her.

"This is only your arraignment for your court date. Today, we will know if you can go home or not until your trial or if you have to stay."

"So, why did I go before the judge before they sent me here?"

"That was only for them to release you here."

Annabelle nodded. "So, there is still a chance I can go home?" he asked.

"Yes, there is," he said.

Annabelle let out a sigh of relief.

"Oh, thank God."

"But, I will warn you, in most cases for murder, your chances are slim to none for making bail."

"With God all things are possible." She smiled. She was feeling a sense of hope and she was ready to go up against Hang 'em High Henry because her God was more powerful and mightier than him. For the next twenty minutes, he asked questions and Annabelle answered them truthfully to him. He wrote more, taking key notes, and when he finished, he looked at Annabelle with a smile.

"From what you're telling me, this is an open and shut case. In the next few minutes, we're going to enter a plea of not guilty. This is only the arraignment and not court. Then sometimes this week I'll get with the prosecutor and shoot for a manslaughter plea."

"And what does that mean, the plea thing?"

"We can go for probation, if they don't like what we're aiming for we can go for maybe a year in prison?"

"A year in prison? I'm not trying to go to prison, this wasn't my fault," she cried, raising her voice. "I just want to go home."

"It's easier said than done, Miss Humphrey. This is not an open and shut case and they are going for murder. If I can get the charges reduced from murder to involuntary manslaughter, it's a chance we can win, but if we don't, that's less jail time than a murder rap."

"Well, I surely hope and pray that we can beat it. I'm sure Jesus didn't bring me this far in my life to go prison," she said and looked at him in his eyes. But for some apparent reason, he wasn't looking like he believed what he was saying himself.

He began writing something on a piece of paper, then he looked up at Annabelle and said, "For now, I will be your appointed lawyer unless you can get your own private attorney."

Annabelle nodded and then asked, "So if I'm unable to get my lawyer before my set court date, you the man?"

"You can say that," he said and then the bailiff called the court to come to order. The proceeding started, and it took all of ten minutes before bail was again denied and Annabelle was escorted back to her cell. Three days later, she got word from Daisy Mae that all of Jamal's assets were frozen and the account that she thought was solely hers was not, so there was no money to afford a private attorney. Having to stick with Mr. Barrett, Annabelle was confident that all would go well, and she just left it all in God's hands.

15

"No! I wasn't raised in the church, it didn't happen until my mother fell ill and God took her away from me for no reason at all. Cancer they say. But I needed to hear it from God, so I began talking with him every day until my friends started calling me crazy. At that point, I started removing myself from the IN crowds and became a loner. I left Augusta, Georgia a little over a year after I graduated from high-school and took a Greyhound bus to Atlanta. From that point, I lived in a women's shelter and joined a pretty decent church, then I found my position as the Sunday school teacher. I loved working with the youth." Annabelle paused, her eyes scanned around the sea of women prisoners and she noticed that she had had their undivided attention. She could feel herself getting emotional, so she covered her mouth with her hand and then removed it again.

"That was until I met a man. The man that my Pastor had warned me about; he knew him so well because they were brothers from the same womb. I should have turned away then. God was trying to tell me something. Instead, I fell into his powerful arms. Honestly, I didn't see anything wrong with falling in love in church. Then at the blink of an eye, I was standing in the courtroom, my eyes were filled with tears, I was frightened. The jury had been deliberating for the last few hours only to find me guilty on all counts. The judge wasn't light on me either. He sentenced me to life in a Georgia State women's prison. And that's when I stopped believing in God." She took a deep breath and listened at the crowd gasp and mumble.

"But, I knew that deep down inside of me, I wasn't that person to give up like that on faith. See, sometimes Jesus will sit us down and we'll get it confused thinking that he has let us down, so I finally got myself together. Even though it took me eight months of mental health evaluations and being in a strip cell with nothing but a paper gown and a Bible. Yes, I went through a deep depression and I was taking all kinds of meds that made me sleep all day long." She paused and took another deep breath and then out of nowhere, a woman in the audience started to clap and then several more came behind her with applause.

Annabelle scanned the crowd, some of them rose to their feet, and the applause grew louder. She smiled, that was her first night in church at Lee Arrendale State prison. It was the biggest and worst women's prison in the state of Georgia and the crimes ranged from the lowest of the low to the highest crimes commit-ted. Annabelle was still standing at the podium in front of the microphone. She leaned in to it and said, "Thank you, and may God bless each and every last one of you." She backed away from the podium and went and sat down on the front row and faced the visitors from one of the churches that came down there to visit the women.

An older white man stood up. He was dressed in a two-piece brown suit. He went to the podium and said into the microphone. "We got to give this young lady another round of applause," he said and began clapping his hands together. The audience clapped along with him and then he said, "We never know what Jesus Christ has in store for us, we might have our own plans and ideas, but He might laugh at it and send us what we need instead of what we want." He raised his hand and then he pointed his finger at a heavy-set dark-skinned woman and said, "You're blessed." He aimed his finger at a white woman with buzzed haircut and told her the same. He went on, pointing his finger at nearly everyone in the audience telling them all that they were blessed. "God touches our lives in remarkable ways and He'll never stop doing it," he then lowered his voice. In a mere whisper, he softly said, "Just stay true to Him; all you have to do is stay true to Him."

"Amen!" Annabelle shouted and stood to her feet. She sat her Bible in the chair and raised both of her hands in the air and started praising the Lord. She squeezed her eyes shut and began praying silently. By the time she opened her eyes and finished her prayer, the ladies were clearing out and heading back to their assigned dorms. It was almost count time when Annabelle picked up her Bible to leave and the chaplain stopped her. "Humphrey," he said.

Annabelle stopped and turned back to him. She looked up at the older white man in a brown suit and he extended his hand out to her. "That was a wonderful testimony you delivered tonight."

"Thank you, I really appreciate that."

"Listen, I'm still a fairly new chaplain here at Lee Arrendale State prison and I think you'll be a great chaplain aid to assist me with getting things in order. What do you say?"

"Well, I've been here for eight months, but this is my first day out in population, and I don't know the ins and outs of the prison yet."

"I'll speak with the warden about you and let him know that I want you to work up here with me. And besides, it'll be better than being in the dorm all day, every day. Try it out for thirty days and if you don't like it, you don't have to come back."

She smiled and said, "Okay."

"Take care, and hopefully you'll be up here in the next few

days," he said and then turned and walked away. Annabelle watched him walk away and then she headed back to her dorm. It was only a three-minute walk and as she headed back, she saw the sparkling razor wire spinning around the top of the fence in the night. She looked up into the night sky at the half moon, it was beautiful. She wished the smell of cow manure wasn't lingering in the air so her walk back would have been more pleasant, however it was better than being in the hole. She wished she still had her freedom but being out of that hole was enough for the moment.

This can't be life my life, she thought to herself as she entered the dorm where she was housed in. On the inside, it was noisy as heck. The TV's were blaring, women were screaming at one another, and there was a lot of laughter in the air. As she approached her cell, she smelled marijuana. Annabelle walked into her cell to find that it was smoked out, there were three other women sitting around smoking a rolled blunt. Annabelle's roommate's hazel eyes landed on her. She was a caramel complexioned sister, very pretty, but apparently not too smart.

"So, you must be my new cellmate?" she asked.

Annabelle started fanning the smoke with her hand and she nodded her head up and down. The pretty girl stood up, dressed in basketball shorts and a white tank top. She pulled on the blunt two short quick times and handed it to one of the other girls that were sitting on her bunk. "I'm Pretty Melissa," she said. "How you doing?"

"I'm doing good, my name is Annabelle." They shook hands for a brief moment, and then Pretty Melissa turned around and introduced her two home girls. The closer one to Annabelle was chubby and she wore state issued glasses and had an afro on top of her head, she stared at Annabelle, her eyes nearly closed from the marijuana. She licked her lips and said, "What up?" Her head went up and came back down.

"Hey," was all Annabelle said.

The other girl stood, towering Annabelle holding the blunt between her fingers. She was at least five, eleven and had wide shoulders. She looked like she could have played in the WNBA with no problem Annabelle thought. She put the blunt to her lips and pulled on it and blew out a stream of smoke directly towards Annabelle's face. She closed her eyes and fanned her hand in front of her face. "Excuse me, but I don't smoke," Annabelle barked.

The tall girl handed off the blunt to the other girl and walked up on Annabelle, standing only inches from her face and she said, "You too pretty to want any kind of smoke wit' a chick like me." Then she put her hand on the back of Annabelle's neck and with a strong powerful yank she pulled her closer, nearly kissing her lips. "You've been in protected custody for eight months playing crazy. But you on compound now, so you're going to get with the program or go back into hiding." Then she kissed her cheek and let her go and stared down at her.

Heart racing, Annabelle stood her ground. Her eyes were on hers when she said, "You never did tell me your name."

The tall girl flashed a smile. "My Man is what they call me," she said.

"Well, I'm not going to call you that," she said and tried to walk around her, but the tall woman swiftly moved in her path. Annabelle looked over at her cellmate Pretty Melissa and said, "Will you please call her off?"

Pretty Melissa must have heard the nervousness in Annabelle's voice, and the fear in her eyes. She stared at her for a long second and Annabelle was staring back at her. "I just want to do what God sent me here to do." Then she easily moved around the tall woman's frame and went to her bunk and started making up her bed. Pretty Melissa gave her friends a head nod and both of them left without saying a word. When the cell door closed, Annabelle looked back at her cellmate and said, "Thank you, your blessings will come."

"Tuh, I heard that a thousand times," she said and flushed the roach of the blunt down the toilet. She grabbed a spray bottle of bleach and a cleaning rag and began wiping the room down to kill the marijuana scent. Then she looked at Annabelle.

"First, let me tell you something. In here, you're gonna either adapt or get eaten. You are red and pretty and these chicks in here are savages, not all of them but the ones that are, they will be at you."

"Be at me? I don't understand what you're saying."

"You just got to be able to hold ya' own in here, they gonna try to get you to pay for protection and they gonna try to get you to do some things that you don't wanna do. Now you get where I'm coming from?"

Annabelle nodded her head, then she asked, "So, what do you suggest that I do?"

"Mind your business, keep doing your Bible thing and never tell the police what's going on back here in the dorms. That's a start," she said and walked over to her bed. She sat down on her bunk and pulled back the top of her mattress, there was a manila envelope underneath it. She pulled it out and sat it on her lap. On the inside of it, she pulled out a homemade knife that was made from a strong piece of metal, it was six inches long with a sharp tip and a handle made from what looked like old threads of sheets, to Annabelle. She held it carefully in her hand and looked up at Annabelle. "You see this? It's my knife, damn near everybody in here got one. I keep it right here under my mattress, if you ever need it and I'm not here, get it and use it if you have to."

Annabelle shook her head. "Thanks, but I don't think I'll need that."

Pretty Melissa put it back underneath her mattress and laid back on her bunk. Annabelle was still making up her bed, the room was silent for a minute, and Pretty Melissa crossed her legs at the ankles while staring up at the bottom of the top bunk. "You know, my home girl that was messing with you is really cool, but she can be serious at times."

"Was she serious a few minutes ago?" Annabelle asked. Then she turned to her locker box that was mounted against the wall where all her clothes were stored. When Annabelle didn't get a response from Pretty Melissa she turned around and looked at her. She was sleep with her mouth wide open, but she wasn't making a sound. Annabelle smiled, thought about the blunt that she'd just smoked, it had finally settled in on her. She shook her head and turned back to her locker box and continued to straighten it up, folding up her clothes and rolling up her socks in nice little neat roles. After she finished getting her locker box in order, she got her towel and cosmetics and slipped her feet into a pair of shower shoes. Annabelle walked over to the sink and looked at herself in the metal mirror that was on the wall just above the sink. She stared at her reflection, noting that she looked like she had aged ten years. The entire ordeal had her tired and mentally drained. "This is my first night here in population, God. I know I'm in real prison now, and I know that it isn't going to be easy. All I ask of you is to watch over me and keep me protected," she prayed to herself.

Then her spirit spoke to her, telling her that she was going to be just fine. That with God, no matter where she was He'd be with her and she felt at the moment that He had put her up in there for a reason and she was going to allow the Holy Spirit to guide her footsteps. There were many there that needed to hear the Word, so she decided if the warden permitted her to work with the chaplain, she'd gladly take the job.

"Okay. Thank you, Father. Your will, not mine," she recited and then she went and took her shower.

The following morning, Annabelle was up bright and early. She was sitting out in the day room area with a hot cup of coffee and her Bible opened to Hebrews chapter four, verse twelve. She began softly reading out loud, "For the word of God is alive and active. Sharper than any double-edge sword, it penetrates even to dividing souls and spirits, joints and marrow; it judges the thought and attitudes of the heart." She sat back and allowed that to sink in for a second. Annabelle was always studying and analyzing the words of the Bible and what they meant. She closed her eyes and meditated on it for a few minutes. She opened her eyes and took a sip from her cup, she then looked around the dorm. It was a few women up and moving around. She noticed two females, cleaning the floors and when she turned her head towards the water fountain, she saw two rough looking females staring directly at her. They both wore khaki pants and white tank tops. One of them was very dark complexioned and had golds across the top row of her teeth. The other girl was built as if she worked out, and her head was nearly shaved bald. She had tattoos on both of her arms from her shoulders to her wrist. She looked back down at her Bible and pretended to be reading. She flipped a few pages and found Psalms and just then she felt a hand touch her on her right shoulder. Annabelle turned around and looked up at the dark-skinned woman with the gold teeth.

"How you doing? Can I sit down wit' cha'?" she asked in a deep southern drawl.

"Of course." Annabelle smiled. The girl sat down on Annabelle's right side and the other girl with the tattoos sat down on the left side of her. The one with the tattoos picked up Annabelle's Bible. She flipped a couple of pages and turned to Leviticus chapter twenty-four, verse seventeen. She then turned the Bible towards Annabelle with her finger on the line that she wanted her to read. "Read it out loud," she ordered.

Annabelle's eyes went down to the verse, and she was hesitant at first, but she read.

"Whoever takes a human life shall surely must be put to death."

"Okay, so you are familiar with an eye for an eye term?"

"Yes, I am. But only God knows my heart and what happened."

Just then, out of nowhere, the girl with the gold teeth swiped Annabelle's Bible off the table sending it clean across the floor and Annabelle jumped. She looked at her and she tried to stand up, but the other girl held her in her seat with her hands on her shoulders.

"Check this out chick. This is strictly blood gang business now. Our family on the street said that you killed they best friend and they want yo' face on a tee shirt, or you can pay for your life."

Just then, the intercom came on and the voice that came through the speakers said, "Annabelle Humphrey, report to the chaplain's office."

"I got to go," Annabelle cried. Her heart was racing, she had no clue what they'd do to her. When the tattooed female released her grip from her shoulders, she quickly stood up and went for her bible. She bent over and picked it up thinking how she was going to handle herself now that she was in prison with real criminals. Annabelle didn't bother to look back as she hurried towards the door. She saw the officer looking at her through the glass.

"Humphrey?" she asked.

Annabelle nodded, and she watched the officer write something down and then she buzzed her through the door. Annabelle turned and backed out of the room with her eyes on the two women that had just threatened her. They were still watching her. She pointed up towards the sky and whispered. "God is good."

16

_T_he chapel in the prison looked almost identical to the inside of a church in the free world, and when Annabelle walked in, she didn't feel like she was locked away. There were twenty rows of wooden pews and lavender colored carpet on the floor. There was an altar up front, and a small pulpit, but there were no windows. Annabelle walked through and made her way through a side door that took her to the next area where there was a hallway and several different cubicles set up like mini offices, each with desk and computers. They were all occupied with counselors and even a few of the inmates. A white female prisoner dressed in all brown stuck her head out when Annabelle walked by.

"Are you, Humphrey?" she asked.

Annabelle turned around. "Yes, ma'am," she said.

She motioned her hand and said, "Come with me." Annabelle went inside of the cubicle that she was in. She extended her hand out in front of Annabelle and she shook it.

"I'm Sarah, and I'm one of the chaplain aids," she said and let her hand go. She walked around to the other side of the desk and sat down in a cushioned swivel chair.

"Have a seat," she said to Annabelle.

Annabelle pulled out the chair that was in front of the desk and sat down. She then sat her Bible on the desk and looked at Sarah while she tapped on the computer keys. Annabelle was amazed because she'd heard so many stories about female prisoners not having any access to computers and things like that. Now she was seeing it first-hand that it was all a lie. Sarah finally looked up at her.

"I heard your testimony in church last night and it was awesome," she said.

"Thank you," Annabelle responded. She looked around the small cubical and then asked, "Is this your office?"

"Something like that, I've been working up here for almost five years, so I've certainly built up my trust around here with the staff and administration. And honestly, it's very rare that the chaplain asks someone himself to become one of his orderlies."

"So, I'll assume that's a good thing."

"What? Do you know how many people be trying to get up here? Okay, first of all, you're not just a chaplain orderly up here. You'll also be working for the captain, the lieutenants, the counselors and probably running a few errands for the warden, from here to the front hall. It's only me and another girl, she's Hispanic. And what they try to do is have a black, a white and a Hispanic up here so everybody will have someone to relate to. And I'm going to be honest with you, by you being new and black, most of the black girls are gonna want to deal with you."

Annabelle thought about the two girls that she had just met and shook her head.

"So, what happened to the last black girl that was working up here?"

"Good question, well she kind of got herself caught up in some mess with the gangs and stuff. She ended up going to the hole and she was transferred to another prison. Don't get me wrong, she was a good girl and had the heart of gold, but it's a whole lot of mess going on back there. And all I can tell you, don't get caught up with the gang bangers."

Annabelle smiled. "I only gang bang for, God," she said.

"Now, I like that saying; I've never heard that one before," Sarah said, and then she added. "So, some of the duties here are mopping, sweeping, emptying the trash, and we will have to dust. Sometimes we may have to go to all the dorms and hang up memos and pass out paperwork. We run copies from the fax machines. Some of the officers may bring us some home cooked food and it'll be days that we'll be eating free world food and not that slop that they feed us in the dining hall. Lastly, we have access to all of the computers back here, but we are not allowed to use social media. At least not under your real name anyway." She winked.

"Got it," she said, "My cellmate already gave me the run down about not telling the officers what goes on in here."

Sarah stood up. "You can leave your Bible in here while I take you on a quick tour."

Annabelle stood up, excited. She was starting to feel a little more comfortable about the entire situation. For the next twenty minutes, Sarah gave her a tour of the area where she would be working. She met some of the officers and staff and some of them seemed pretty cool. The rest of the day went by fast and smooth, but in the back of her mind, she knew that she had to go back to the dorm where she had to face the arising problem from earlier that morning.

By the time she got back to her dorm it was nearly eight o'clock at night. She was tired and was ready to take her shower and go to sleep. When she got inside her cell, the first thing she noticed was Pretty Melissa had moved out, her mattress was gone, and all of her visible personal belongings were gone. Annabelle opened up her wall locker and saw that it was empty. Something wasn't right, she thought to herself and she wondered what happened. Annabelle sat her Bible down on the desk that sat in the corner and then unlocked her combination lock that she had on her wall locker. When she finally got it opened, her mouth dropped when she noticed that all her stuff was gone, no clothes, no food, no hygiene products, no letters, no legal material, nothing. She stood there frozen for a few minutes dumbfounded. Seconds later, the door to her cell opened and when she turned to see who had entered, it was the tattooed chick from earlier. She had two net bags filled with food, clothes and other material.

"Well, I see we meet again. I'm your new cellmate," she announced. She walked all the way inside and stopped directly in front of Annabelle and sat her bags down.

Annabelle stared at her for few seconds before she asked, "What happened to my stuff?"

The other woman turned around and went to close the cell door. Then she politely walked back up to Annabelle and with one swift motion she grabbed Annabelle's neck and forcefully shoved her up against the wall in the back of the cell. Annabelle's head hit the wall with a thud. "Let me tell you somethin'." She wrinkled her nose and growled. "If you want this blood pressure you can get it."

Annabelle was trying to wiggle out of her grip, but the girl was too strong for her, her eyes watered, and she stared into the eyes of a devilish woman who was not friendly at all. She let her grip go from Annabelle's neck and stepped back from her and got in a fighting stance like she was ready to go a round or two with Annabelle, but Annabelle didn't move. Annabelle coughed to catch her breath and wiped the tears that ran from her eye.

The tattooed bully shook her head and chuckled and then went to the door. She went for her rolled up mattress that was just outside the door and she walked back in and placed it on the empty bunk. After that, she proceeded to unpack her bags, while Annabelle was still standing there too terrified to move. She tried to calm herself down by taking a couple of long deep breaths. She was angry that she wasn't physically strong enough to tackle her new cellmate and she hoped that she would not make her life a living hell.

The girl turned around and picked up her other net bag and she dumped everything out on her bed. It was food and cosmetics and other personal items.

"I know all your stuff got stolen but I'm going to give you something until you get on your feet."

Annabelle remembered some of the horror stories that she heard through the walls while she was in the hole. *Don't take nothing from nobody in prison because it's always a hidden fee.*

Your life ain't worth nothing more than a Butterfinger candy bar.

Don't get caught up with them gang members.

Annabelle shook her head. "No, thank you, I'm good. I don't need anything from you." And with that being said, she climbed up on her bunk fully dressed. She couldn't brush her teeth or wash her face because she didn't have a toothbrush or nothing. She was lying on her back, just staring at the ceiling and started praying silently to herself until she finally drifted off to sleep.

The following morning, Annabelle woke up just a little past six a.m. She sat up her bunk, rubbed her eyes and looked around. The room was dark, she looked down to see if her cellmate was sleep. She was, tucked underneath the covers and everything. Annabelle eased down out of the bed, still fully dressed. She walked over to the sink and rinsed her mouth out with some water and sprinkled some over her face to try to wake up a little and then she relieved her bladder on the cold stainless-steel toilet after covering it with tissue paper. After she washed her hands, she looked back at her cellmate again and realized that she didn't even know her name. Annabelle would normally start her morning off with a hot cup of coffee and a prayer, but since all of her stuff had been stolen, all she could do was get on her knees at the foot of the bed and say a prayer. It didn't take her long to finish, and just as she was getting up, her cellmate was getting up also. She flipped the covers back and sat up, her feet hit the floor and she slipped them into a pair of Nike slides and stood up and stretched and yarned. When she looked at Annabelle, she said, "It's good waking up to a pretty face every morning." Then she playfully smacked her on her butt and went to the toilet.

"Please, don't disrespect me like that anymore," she said and walked out of the room and closed the door behind her. When she got out into the day room of the dormitory, she looked around, saw a bunch of faces, but everyone was minding their own business. She stood there in front of her cell for a moment, feeling the dirt from yesterday on her body and the taste of bad breath in her mouth. Her tongue felt thick and sticky and all she wanted was some mouthwash. Annabelle tried to get past her irritation and then noticed an older woman with salt and pepper hair waving her hand in the air, asking Annabelle to come over. Without hesitation, she walked over towards the old lady and tried to give a smile, but it wasn't authentic because on the inside, Annabelle was hurting emotionally from the situation that she was in. "Yes, ma'am," Annabelle said.

"Where you from?" was the first question that the old lady asked her.

"Well, I'm originally from Augusta, but I've been living in Atlanta for the last few years."

"Augusta! That's interesting, I'm from Augusta also," she turned around and told Annabelle to follow her, and she followed her to her cell. The old lady turned on the light and went and sat down on her bunk while Annabelle stood at the door close enough to run out just in case it was some kind of setup or trap. "You can relax a little," the old woman said.

"It's not that easy," Annabelle responded. "I'm on high alert around here. All my stuff has been stolen, they trying to make me pay and everything," she shrugged her shoulders and lowered her head. "I just don't know," she said sadly. "I think I'm just gonna go back to the hole until I get transferred or something."

The old lady just sat quietly and listened to Annabelle until she finished. "I'm on my fourteenth year straight," she finally said. "And out of all my years, ain't nan' one of these broads never ran me from compound. And you don't need to let them run you back to the hole either. Stand up for yourself now, if you have to fight, go ahead and fight. If you get yo' butt beat. So, what? You fought. Respect has to be earned around here. In this world baby, you can either be the chess player or a chess piece. Remember that. Now what high-school you went to in Augusta?"

"Laney," she said proudly.

The old lady cocked her head to the side a little, her eyes squinted a little.

"Are you serious? I went to Laney, too. I didn't get a chance to graduate because I been in and out the system all my life. I got my GED though." She stuck her little fat hand out towards Annabelle and said, "My name's Rose, they call me Gangsta Granny in this damn prison though."

Annabelle smiled. "Gangsta Granny, that's cute, but Miss Rose sounds so much better to me, how old are you?"

"I'm grown damnit, that's all that matters." She stood up, stared Annabelle dead in her eyes. "What cho' mama name is?"

Annabelle froze from the question, now her eyes seemed to be going from side to side as she looked at Rose. "Demetrius, but everybody called her Dot."

Rose put her hands on her waist and twisted up her face. "Dot?" she nearly yelled. "Stayed on ninth street, yellow house next to the church that burned down?"

"Yes, that's where we lived. That's my mama. God bless the dead."

Rose's mouth fell open. "Dot dead? Are you serious, from what?"

"Cancer, and she used to drink really bad also."

"Honey, I knew yo' damn mama like the back of my hand. Yo'

mama use to be real pretty before them drugs and stuff and that boy put that damn stuff in her drank at the cool spot one night."

"Wait, what happened?" Annabelle asked interested in any and everything Rose knew about her mom.

"Yeah honey, see back in the days yo' mama had got caught up wit' dis' ole fake pimp out of Detroit that called himself Dirty Red. Yeah, that was his name. He got mad at yo' mama cause she didn't wanna work in the streets no mo'." She paused and took a deep breath like she was getting angry just by thinking about it.

Annabelle listened and frowned all at the same time.

"What do you mean by working in the streets no more?" she asked.

Rose put her hand up to her lips. "I'm sorry, honey; I might be talking too much."

"No, it's alright, for years I've been wanting to know the side about my mother that I never knew, like I've heard bits and pieces but I really wanna know."

Rose took a deep breath, then she pointed at the stool that was attached to the desk.

"Grab a seat," she said.

Annabelle looked at the chair first, then she moved over towards it and sat down. Rose sat back down on the foot of her bed and put her elbows on her knees and looked at Annabelle.

"Dot was a heroin addict, and Dirty Red was the reason behind it all, he was pimpin' her out. And when she didn't wanna work no mo', he slipped somethin' in her drink that drove her crazy. It was to the point where she used to walk the streets talking to herself. But before that I can definitely tell you this. Yo' mama didn't play in the streets. She was a fighter and she had a crew of girls that was under her that was just as crazy. But I also heard that she had got herself together and got into the Bible and got saved and everything by the time you came along," she said. "But I was back in prison when that happened, and I lost contact with the streets."

"So, you heard my mama had got saved and got herself together?" she asked with bright eyes.

Rose nodded her head and then, someone knocked at the door, the both of them looked up and Annabelle saw her cellmate standing there. She was cracking her knuckles and told Annabelle to come to her.

"I'm talking right now," Annabelle said, "Give me a few minutes." Then she turned her head back towards Rose. "Like I was saying..."

Her cellmate smiled and turned around and walked away. "Now, that B is a problem, I try my best not to cuss, but you gonna have to hurt that girl or she gonna hurt you."

"I kind of figured that, but I'm not trying to get into any more trouble than I'm already in."

"How much time you got?"

"Well, the Judge sentenced me to a life sentence, but according to the good Lord..."

"Look, let me tell you something," Rose cut her off and stood. She walked over to the door and looked out through the square sheet of glass. She saw the girl waiting at the table for Annabelle to come out. She then turned around and faced Annabelle. Staring at her face she said, "I know you're not built for this, and these women up in here will destroy you. These broads fight dirty and have no mercy. I'm an old woman, but I can handle it for you. At least I can get her out of the dorm, the same way they got your first cellmate out of the dorm. My two options are mix up this hot water and baby oil and dash it in her face or I can say she tryin' to make me perform sexual acts on her and they gonna put me and her in the hole until further notice."

Annabelle smiled, but it was weak. "Miss Rose, I honestly appreciate you trying to help me, but I think that this is something that I need to handle myself."

"How honey? She is the head of their lil gang. But it's a lot of them running around here. If you don't strike first, you won't make it past two weeks around here."

"Miss Rose, do you believe in God?" Annabelle asked her.

"Yes, I do. But baby, let me tell you something, this is a real-life savage that you're dealing with."

"And that's why I asked you to say a prayer for me. I'm sure God has his hands in this situation." She let her hands go and gave Rose a hug. "Thank you for everything and I'm more than grateful for all that you shared with me about my mother." She kissed her cheek and separated from her and walked towards the door.

"I'm about to go to my detail now, so I'll probably see you later tonight or in the morning." She turned around and left.

Annabelle walked out into the dormitory and walked straight to her room, she grabbed her Bible from her desk and when she was about to leave, her cellmate was coming in and closed the door behind her. Before she could say something, Annabelle said, "What do I have to pay you to keep me safe around here?"

The girl walked up close to Annabelle and put her hands around Annabelle's waist, their faces were only inches apart from one another. "Let's start with a kiss."

"I haven't even brushed my teeth this morning nor have I had a shower. And it's time for me to go to my detail, and I don't even know your name."

"Everybody calls me Five-Star round here," she purred and then her hands eased down to the curve of Annabelle's butt. Annabelle eased away from her in a playful manner. "Let me get out of here and get to my detail. We will definitely talk later," Annabelle said, then she gave her a quick peck on her cheek and went towards the door and then paused. "I'll see you later, okay?" Annabelle said, but she knew in her mind that she wasn't returning back to this dorm or to that room.

hen Annabelle arrived at her detail area, she went into the chapel. It was quiet and peaceful, and no one was in there. The scent of jasmine air freshener lingered in the air and she took a deep breath as she slowly walked down the carpeted isle. She stopped at the altar and then went down on her knees. She sat her Bible down next to her and wedged her fingers in between one another and bowed her head.

"Good morning, Father God. I come to you in prayer asking you to strengthen my mind, body and spirit. I am weary, no Lord a better word is stressed. Please grant me peace Lord, God and continue to walk with me. I'm not trying to be caught up in this mess and if anyone knows that I'm truthful is you. I pray that I walk in complete confidence today knowing that you are with me. Amen."

She sat there for a minute with her head bowed and eyes closed in hopes of God responding back to her like he'd done before. But after five minutes had passed and she heard nothing, she opened her eyes and stood to her feet. She looked around and the chapel was still completely empty. She took a deep breath and headed through the side door that led her to the back where the offices and cubicles were. She walked into the cubicle where Sarah was sitting behind the desk looking like she worked there instead of her being an inmate.

"Good morning," Annabelle said and then took a seat. Annabelle was dying to tell her that that may be her last day, but she couldn't find the right choice of words. She felt her chest tighten and small beads of sweat formed on her forehead. Sarah looked at her.

"Hey, what's wrong? You look petrified."

Annabelle just shook her head from side to side, even though she wanted to breakdown and cry. Not able to conceal her true emotions, tears began to fall from her eyes and she wiped her face with the back of her hand. She took a deep breath to calm herself, then she said, "I'm just having issues with a few people down at my dorm and I'm not trying to get myself into any trouble."

Sarah stood up and walked around to the front of the desk where Annabelle was sitting, and she stood in front of her. She placed her hand on her shoulder.

"I'm so sorry that you have to go through this."

Annabelle just dropped her head down and covered her face with one hand.

"I just don't know what to do," she cried in her hands. Sarah got her some Kleenex and handed them to her and Annabelle wiped her face. They sat silently for a minute until she had stopped crying. She looked up at Sarah and patted her eyes dry. Then she stood up.

"If I don't make it back, I'll be in the hole. Will you send me some food and cosmetics once I get back there?"

"You damn right I will," Sarah said nodding.

Annabelle gave her a quick hug and just that fast, she had made her mind up. She turned and headed back through the chaplain area, and when she got ready to go through the exit door, someone pulled it open from the other side. It was three women prisoners and they were happy and laughing amongst themselves. The first girl was short and stocky, she resembled a bulldog with a bunch of tattoos on her face and although the first two women walked on by, the last girl brushed up against her. Annabelle didn't even bother looking at her, she was already having enough problems, so she just clutched her Bible and kept moving until she heard somebody call out her name. Her heart dropped into the pit of her stomach, but she turned to the sound. Annabelle looked at the stranger and thought she knew her but couldn't quite figure it out from where.

"I been lookin' fo' you," she yelled and began walking towards her. The other two girls had also come back out of the door and was following her. Annabelle braced herself as the women got closer. Then she said, "How in the hell you don't remember me? This Black Girl from the women's shelter in Atlanta," she said with her hands up, arms open and a silly grin on her face.

Annabelle took a deep breath and stared. "Angel!" she said when recognition dawned.

"Yes, and what the world are you doing in prison?" she asked.

"It's a long story, Angel. And right now, I got a situation to go handle," she said taking steps backwards.

"Hold up," Angel said and then turned to her girls. She introduced Annabelle to them. "These are my road dawgs right here," she said. Then she pointed to the tall red girl. "This is Kisha. Kisha, this is Annabelle, y'all remember when I told y'all about the praying girl at the shelter when I was stealing all them damn clothes."

"Girl, you done told us so many stories, I don't remember," Kisha said.

"Well, anyway, shawty like my lil sistah." Then she pointed to the girl that looked like the bulldog. "This Boo. Boo, this is Annabelle."

Annabelle shook the other two girl's hands. "Nice to meet y'all."

"Where are you 'bout to go? We need to sit down and talk for a minute, catch up."

"Well, actually I was about to go fight my roommate."

Angel frowned. "Hold up, come on let's talk for a second." She turned and went through the door that led them to the chaplain area. All four of them sat down on the back row in the chapel, it was still empty except for the four of them. Annabelle and Angel sat next to one another. "Now, talk to me, tell me what's going on?"

Annabelle took a deep breath.

"Okay, right now it's this chick that goes by the name Five Star. She says some people on the outside want me to pay for Jamal's death and she has been making things really bad for me. I think she stole all of my personal stuff and now she wants me to be more than just her cellmate," she said and went on for the next twenty minutes telling Angel the entire story, including how she got there.

"I really don't suppose to get in the Blood gang business, but since you my fam..." She winked. "And I'm Crip to the bone, I'll handle that chick fa ya', so no worries."

Boo interrupted with, "We can go down to the dorm with you and handle this. Ain't no need to wait."

"Nah, I got a better idea. You said you work up here right?" Angel asked.

Annabelle nodded her head.

"Cool, her real name is Lisa Rhodes. Tell the white girl that you work wit' to call her up front to the counselor area. And when she gets here, I'm going to talk to her about the situation, and then I'm gonna get you moved in the dorm with us so you can get some peace and do your legal work and your Bible study and stuff."

They stood and hugged and then Annabelle headed to the office areas to talk to Sarah. Sarah agreed without hesitation and Annabelle breathed a sigh of relief.

Twenty minutes later, Five Star walked in through the double doors alone and was faced with Black Girl, Boo and Kisha. Five Star's face frowned immediately when they surrounded her, she looked from one to the other. "Who wants smoke?" she asked and folded her arms across her chest. She braced herself and flipped her head from one to the other.

"This ain't really 'bout no smoke," Black Girl said while looking in her eyes.

"However, we know you Blood gang just as well as you know we Crippin'. And the only minor situation that we have is my lil cuz, Annabelle. I know you know who I'm talkin' 'bout, right?"

Five Star nodded and then tucked her bottom lip underneath her top row of teeth, then she let out a laugh. "So, she yo' cousin? That lil sweet red thang is my cellmate. But how do I know that you tellin' the truth about her being yo' family."

"Cause my mama called me and told that she was here," Black Girl lied smooth as baby oil, never taking her eyes off Five Star's.

Five Star let out a, "hmph," before she nodded her head. Her eyes darted between the three women, and then she said, "Aw'ight, that's yo' cousin, I feel you. But she still a civilian. I was just gonna bring her home."

"She already home, and I'm here to let you know that I will go to war behind her."

Five Star threw her hands up in the air and smiled at her as if she didn't want any problems, then before she turned around and walked away, she said. "I hear ya' talkin'." Then she walked out of the door.

Then Boo said, "She cannot be trusted."

Black Girl walked towards the door that led towards the hallway where Annabelle was waiting just on the other side of the door. When it came opened, Black Girl gave her a hug and said, "That's handled, now I need you to get with the chaplain ASAP and let him know that you want to come to B unit. Get on that now so you can be moved today."

"You just don't know how much I appreciate that, Angel. I can never repay you."

"Well, if I need you, I'll come to you. Now, go ahead and handle that," she said and then walked out. Just like that, Annabelle's prayers had been answered and she felt like her load had been lifted.

ॐ

A FEW WEEKS HAD GONE BY AND ANNABELLE WAS GETTING MORE comfortable with her new living situation. Every Tuesday and Thursday she was in the law library faithfully working on her case, desperately trying to find some loopholes that would eventually get her case overturned.

That morning the library was quiet, she was sitting at a desk with a stack of books and her transcripts from trial. With a yellow highlighter, she illuminated a sentence that the district attorney said.

"Hands down, this woman murdered a man in cold blood and she has no remorse." Annabelle stared at that sentence for a long time, and it had her in her feelings. It was hurtful as hell and when it was said, she looked back at Pastor James and his mother and saw the hurt and grief on their faces and she just turned back around and listened as the DA drag her name through the mud. She shook her head and snapped back to reality. She looked back over her transcripts, scanning through it for errors. Then she picked up her pen and pulled her notepad in front of her and she began writing something that didn't have anything to do with her case. And her first sentence went like this: *I was standing in my mama's kitchen, it was hot for two reasons, one, we didn't have an air condition; and two, the oven was on with a ham baking inside. The aroma was wonderful, it had my stomach growling and my mouth watering. My mother was standing over the stove frying fatback and chopped onions, the collard greens was on simmer, she wiped her hands* on her apron and said to me. "Daughter, I love you." She never turned around, her back was to me, but she was now putting the fatback and onions in the pot with the collards. That made me smile, I walked over to her and wrapped my arms around her waist and laid my head against her back and I whispered. "I love you. too, Mama."

"Have you made the sweet tea yet?" she asked.

I pressed my head against my mother's back even harder, this was a moment that I had to enjoy, then I pulled away from her and said. "No ma'am, but I'm about to do it now." I went to the counter and pulled down the Dixie Crystal sugar bag and the box of tea, then there was a knock at the front door. "I'll get it, mama," I said to my mother and walked from the kitchen and through the hallway, our floors were made of wood but with every step I took, the floors creaked. When I got to the living room, I saw a man standing on the front porch, the wooden door was opened and the only thing that separated him and me was the screen on the raggedy screen door. When I got to the front door, I noticed that I hadn't never seen the man before around the neighborhood. I stared at him from head to toe. He had a big tall nappy afro and a beard that was thick and nappy as well, his shirt was dirty, the top three buttons were opened, he wore a dingy pair of corduroy pants in the summer, and when I looked down at his feet I noticed that he was barefooted. At the age of twelve, I didn't know what to say or think. My eyes went up to his and I said, "How are doing, sir?"

"Well, I'm doing; I'm here. It took me a minute, but I've finally came."

I was confused as to what he was saying. And I guess it was showing on my face. He then said to me. "May I have something to drink?"

Before I could answer, I heard my mama yell, "Who is it, daughter?"

I turned around and went back into the kitchen where my mama was standing, she was facing me. "It's a man, mama, he only wants something to drank," I said to her.

My mama stared down at me, I noticed that her eyes had

*narrowed, and from years of knowing my mama, that was a sign of
her about to get mad.*

*"Fix him a glass of water," she said and walked up the hallway and
into the living room. She saw him standing there in front of the screen
door. Their eyes met for one second and it seemed as if something had
washed over her. She pushed the screen door open. "Come on in," she
said to him.*

*The man walked in, stood there at the threshold for a moment and
looked around the front room, the furniture was covered with thick
plastic, on the wooden coffee table were some pictures in frames. To the
left was an open window with a box shaped fan sitting inside of it spinning and cooling off the front room. He then looked at her and put out a
huge dirty hand in her face. "Thank you for welcoming me into
your home."*

"You're welcome."

*I was coming around the corner with the ice-cold glass of water
and a paper towel. My mama always told me that I should use a paper
towel when I fixed something to drank just in case the glass started to
sweat. When I finally got into the living room, I saw my mama and the
man shaking hands. She must already know him from somewhere.
Then I heard him say. "I'm God, I was just in the neighborhood
checking on my children. And I must say, this is the seventh house that
I stopped at today. And you are the first person to let me in." Then he
looked at me and said, "I didn't make a mistake when I created you, I'm
not going to stand here and tell you that life is going to be a piece of
cake for you. But I will most defiantly see you through it."*

Annabelle reread what she'd just wrote and tore the paper
from the notepad and balled it up and sat it on the desk in front
of her. She took a deep breath and put her elbows up on the desk,
feeling frustrated. I got to get this case overturned. I got to go
home. This can't be life. She finally looked around the library,
most of the women had their heads buried in their legal material
or glued to the computer screen looking over cases that was
similar to their own. Annabelle buried her hands in her face, she

felt a small headache coming on. She then started getting her stuff together. It was block movement, and that meant that basically everyone had to move at the same time around the prison. When she stood up, she got in line and waited for it to start moving. She noticed the front cover of a magazine that said: Let God Use You. She nodded her head and said to herself, *It's been that way majority of my life.* When she left out of the library, it was nine forty-five in the morning and she went back up to the front hall where she was working on her detail at. When she got through the door, she saw one of the female counselors, she was in her late forties and always stayed dolled up in the latest fashion clothes and shoes, her perfume left a trail through the hallways and you could always tell that she was coming by the way her heels clicked against the tile floors. "Annabelle," she said with a smile.

"Good morning, Counselor Eubanks," she said back. "I see you looking good as usual."

"Aw chile, this ain't nothing," she said, then she touched her on the back of her elbow and said, "Come to my office for a second." She turned and walked off, her heels click-clacking as she went, and Annabelle was following right behind her and into her office. "Close the door," she said to Annabelle and went and sat down behind her desk. Annabelle closed the door and took a seat and faced her. "A lady called here yesterday and asked about you. First, she said she was your auntie, but by the time we got off the phone she said she was your grandmama."

Annabelle smiled. "Was her name, Daisy Mae?"

Counselor Eubanks smiled, her teeth were even and white. "So, you already know who I'm talking about?"

"Yes, actually we aren't related by blood but she's a member of the church that I was at and she took me in from the shelter when I was staying in Atlanta."

Counselor Eubanks stared at Annabelle for a moment, then her eyes went to the computer screen and then shifted back to her. "I didn't know that you were serving a life sentence." Her mouth was slightly parted open, and her head was moving side to side. "If you don't mind me asking, what happened? You most certainly don't seem like the type of person that's supposed to be in here; especially with all that time."

Annabelle cleared her throat and pulled her chair up a little bit until her elbows was resting on her desk. "Sometimes, my situation overwhelms me just as it did for the court system and the church that I use to be a part of. When I got to Atlanta, I joined a church in Decatur and I became the Sunday school teacher. I wind up in a quick relationship with the pastor's younger brother. He was more of the financial backer for the church, but he also had his secrets that nobody else in the church knew about. So, he showered me with gifts, big gifts like a Porsche and expensive clothes, but he did something that I didn't respect."

"And what was that?"

"He got me high on a date rape drug and recorded me having sex with him. I wasn't aware of it until the other girl got mad at him for whatever reason and she exposed him, she sent me some of the video to my phone. I checked him about the situation and just wanted to leave. But it wasn't that easy, he hit me, fractured my jaw." She rubbed her face in a slow motion, it was a memory that she hated reliving, but it was in her. "He had me out in the cabin house in north Georgia somewhere, and he went to sleep, and I tried to escape, I went downstairs and got a knife because I needed something to pry the lock off with, I didn't get it to kill him. Anyway, he came downstairs and caught me trying to get out the door, I turned around with the knife in my hand." She paused, her eyes were beginning to tear up. Counselor Eubanks handed her some Kleenex napkins and she pulled a few out for herself. They were both looking at one another and wiping tears from their eyes. Annabelle went on. "I stabbed him in the leg, I was only trying to get away and not to hurt him. After that..." Her heart was feeling like it was being squeezed. "My God knows I didn't mean it." She broke down in tears.

Counselor Eubanks got up from her chair and came around the desk where Annabelle was, and she gave her a woman to woman hug. "It's alright, baby" she whispered in her ear. She rocked side to side with Annabelle as if she was trying to rock a baby to sleep. "I didn't mean to do it, I swear I didn't. No one believes me, and my entire church turned their backs against me, even my Pastor. They think I'm some kind of monster and it hurts like hell. The only person from the church that still writes me and supports me is the lady that called you."

She finally pulled back and Annabelle looked her in her face and saw that she was crying harder than she cried. Annabelle got a dry Kleenex and wiped the counselor's face for her, after a few minutes of silence, the counselor sat back down and looked at the computer screen and told Annabelle, "I'm going to put her down on your visitation list as your grandmother because you don't have anybody listed as a next of kin or nothing." She paused and started typing something on the computer, she looked back at Annabelle. "When was the last time you saw her?" she asked.

"She was at the trial, the only person that was cheering for me to win. She's such a sweetheart."

Counselor Eubanks dabbed her wet eyes again and said, "Annabelle, whatever you do, don't lose your faith, don't stop praying because we all know that God can move mountains."

"Thank you, Miss. Eubanks and I really appreciate your help and support." She crossed her hands and placed them both over her heart, the pain was still there, the hurt was oozing through her pores and it was displayed all over her face.

"Don't thank me, baby. I want to see you get out of here, we are claiming that. You don't deserve this."

Annabelle stood up. "Well, let me at least look like I'm doing something. I'm about to go clean the windows and sweep and mop the floors."

Counselor Eubanks leaned in and whispered, "Do you have any money on your account?"

"No," Annabelle whispered. "But I don't want you to get in any trouble, so I'm good right now," she said and then turned and walked out the door.

18

*L*ater that evening, Annabelle and Black Girl were in the dorm sitting at one of the tables in the day room area. A few of the other women were watching *Love and Hip-Hop* reruns. Although Annabelle didn't care for Black Girl's conversations about a getting money scheme, or making moves on a quick hustle, getting rich quick and the gang life she was a cool inmate. She was thirty-three years old with one son and doing what they were all doing; living day to day. However, since her and Annabelle had reunited, she was getting more and more interested in God and learning about the Word of God.

"While you were gone today, I did read a lil' somethin' from the Bible," Black Girl confessed with a little smirk.

A huge grin was plastered across Annabelle's face.

"Seriously, what did you read?" she asked.

"I just read a lil somethin' 'bout Samson and Delilah; how he went out trickin' and he bumped into Delilah, and when he got the good he fell in love. She was just like a typical broad in the streets on some sneak tip with the man who wanted to take him down. But he was so hooked on shawty that he told her that his strength was never taking a razor to his head after he kept taking out ole boy armies. Samson really had me in my feelings because he trusted shawty, but she betrayed him and caused him to lose his gift from the Big Man upstairs. But what had me is when the Man upstairs still came and restored him, and he still took out his enemies. That like gave me hope, like even when you fail, God still will come fo' ya and have yo' back." She paused and then said, "He got them lames at the end, even though he took himself outta the game, God let me come back on they as—I mean butts."

Annabelle was impressed at how she interpreted the story in her own way of understanding it.

"I like the way you broke that down, Angel," she said.

"Well, I appreciate that. Other than that, did everything go pretty smooth today up front?"

Annabelle shrugged her shoulders. "I went to the law library this morning and worked on my case a little bit, but I got side-tracked and started working on a story about this old man that knocked on the door of this little girl's house, who lived with her mom and he said he was God."

"Now, that sounds interesting, if I was you I would write that sh— I mean stuff. You might get in Oprah's book club, make some millions and buy yo' way up out this raggedy prison."

Annabelle laughed. "You are hilarious, you know that?"

"Girl, I'm serious. This Bible thang is your callin'. You already got a way wit' words," she said, and then added. "As long as it ain't your life story about yo' case, you good."

"I'll write it if you come with me."

"Come with you where?" Black Girl asked with a confused look on her face.

"I need a sister in Christ to walk this next level with me."

"So, you basically want me to get saved? I can't do that right now, see around here, they think everybody that be reading the Bible is soft and be using it to keep the wolves off they butts."

"But everybody already knows you're not soft, Angel. You get the utmost respect around here."

Black Girl shook her head slowly. "Nah, you don't understand. It ain't that easy." Her eyes locked in straight on Annabelle.

"But you do believe in God, right?"

"Oh, without a doubt. I did go to church when I was a lil girl, and I sang in the choir and everything. My big mama used to put all that damn Vaseline on my face and I had to wear this big ugly dress every Sunday, the same one." She laughed at the thought of it. "Maybe that's why I don't like church, I'm not sure." She shrugged her shoulders.

Annabelle laughed out loud while shaking her head at the same time. "But you are a full-grown woman now and..."

Black Girl cut her off, "Listen shawty, you like a lil sistah' to me. But right now, I got to keep my eyes peeled for these haters. I know they plottin' and watchin'. You walk yo' path with God, and I'm gonna have to Crip-walk mine. And besides, God knew what he was doing when he made us cross paths."

Annabelle sat quietly for a moment, then she said, "Well, tonight before you go to bed, be sure to read Psalms twenty-three, okay."

"Okay, and make sure you write that story." She stood and put out a balled fist and Annabelle balled up her fist and touched hers.

"I'm on it." Annabelle smiled. She stood and headed to take a shower. After she ate some Ramen noodles, said her prayers and went to sleep.

❦

THE NEXT MORNING, ANNABELLE WAS UP BRIGHT AND EARLY AND ON her knees, as always praying and talking to God. She needed the peace and tranquility that it brought to her. After she'd finished praying, she got up and got herself together and within the next hour she was on her way up to the front hall where her detail was at. When she arrived, the first thing that she did was go to the closet and remove the dust mop and began sweeping the floors from top to bottom. Pushing the wide broom up and down the hallway, after about fifteen minutes went by, she saw Counselor Eubanks go into her office. Annabelle didn't say anything to her because she didn't want the rest of the staff to think that they had had something going on. They used the phrase 'personal dealings' a lot in the prison system and that was something that she didn't want. She finally went back to the closet, and she put the dust mop up and removed the mop bucket and the mop that was hanging from a hook on the wall. She filled the bucket up with water and touched up the floors, and just as she was passing by Counselor Eubanks' office with the mop, she heard, "Annabelle, come here for a minute." Annabelle paused for a second, she closed her eyes and opened them slowly. That was the last thing she wanted, but she decided to get it over with.

"One second, let me put this mop away," Annabelle said.

On that note, Counselor Eubanks stuck her head out of her office. "Annabelle, come on, hurry," she whispered, waving for her to come in quickly.

Annabelle pulled the mop and bucket into the office with her and closed the door behind her. "Good morning," Annabelle said.

Counselor Eubanks was already behind her desk by the time she shut the door. She opened the top right drawer on her desk and pulled out a small breakfast sandwich that was wrapped in aluminum foil and handed it to her. "I thought about you when I was making breakfast this morning, it's turkey sausage, eggs and cheese. Go ahead and eat it and trust me. It tastes better than the dining hall food."

Annabelle didn't waste any time unwrapping it. She quickly

bit into it and chewed it with her eyes closed. It was indeed delicious, and she was trying to enjoy every bite of the delicious breakfast sandwich. She truly missed real home cooked food. While she ate the still warm sandwich, Counselor Eubanks was doing something on her computer. Within a few seconds she started laughing.

Annabelle was on her last bite, although she wanted to take it slow, she knew that time was of the essence. After it was gone, she grabbed the napkin that Miss Eubanks had on her desk and wiped her hands and mouth.

"You don't know how much I appreciated that delicious breakfast sandwich. Thank you so much."

She waved her hand dismissively at Annabelle, then she laughed again.

"Don't mention it," she said and continued to giggle.

"What is so funny?" Annabelle inquired.

"These people on Facebook be acting up early in the morning. Come around here and look at this," she said to Annabelle. Annabelle walked around to the other side of the desk and stood next to the counselor and peered at the screen. When she looked at the meme that said: God has no phone, but I still talk to him. He has no Facebook, but He still my friend. He does not have a twitter, but I still follow Him.

Annabelle read it and really didn't see anything funny about it. She looked at Counselor Eubanks. "I don't get it how that is funny," she said.

"It's not the post, my home girl posted this but it's the comments underneath it. She pointed her finger at the first comment and Annabelle leaned in closer and looked at it. It read: Lady please, we been friends three years on Facebook, and every time your baby daddy doesn't show up, you start posting memes about God. Get a life. Lol.

Annabelle smiled, but it wasn't really funny to her still. But she played her part and laughed anyway. The counselor then asked her, "Do you have a Facebook page?"

That caught Annabelle off guard, she thought about it for a second.

"No, I actually never had one."

Counselor Eubanks looked at Annabelle with a surprised expression over her face.

"Are you serious? Everybody and they mama have a Facebook page, or at least had one once upon a time. Let me guess, you on Instagram right."

Annabelle shook her head.

"Listen at me," she whispered. "On Facebook, you can find old friends that you haven't seen or spoken to since elementary school, the page doesn't have to be in your name. And I'm sure it's someone out there in the free world that would love to hear from you."

"It might be, Counselor Eubanks. But honestly, I don't really have any friends like that."

"Well, I'm going to create you one anyway." She pointed towards the door. "Look out there and make sure ain't none of the unit managers, wardens or nobody out there."

Annabelle took the mop, she opened the door and pretended to be mopping the front of the office and outside the door, she looked left, and then right. She saw the old white mental health counselor turn the corner going in the opposite direction. Annabelle went back into the office and closed the door. "It's clear," she said.

"Good, now what would be a good name for your page?" she asked.

"Honestly, I don't know."

"Okay, I see that you don't seemed too interested so we don't have to bother with it." Then out of nowhere, something flashed into her head, Annabelle asked, "Do people write stories on there?"

"Baby, people do whatever on Facebook, with the right topic you can reach the world."

"Name my page The Sunday School Teacher," she said with a little bit more enthusiasm. She walked around the desk and stood next to her counselor and looked down at the computer screen.

"The Sunday School Teacher! I really like that." She began typing. Then she said, "Now, you know that you can't have any pictures of yourself on here. That'll be a dead giveaway."

"I don't really need any pictures, maybe some praying hands or something." She said anxiously.

"That sounds like a great idea, so I guess you gonna be writing about the Bible and stuff like that."

"Yes, I actually had a story that I started writing but I threw it in the trash, but I can rewrite it and put it on my page. But how will people notice it if I don't have any friends?"

Counselor Eubanks was still typing, creating the email for her page. Then she said to Annabelle. "First, let's create your bio. Where are you from?"

"God," she said.

"Humph, I love it." She typed it in, then she asked, "Where do you want me to say you live at now?"

"I live with Christ," Annabelle said, her heart was pumping faster. That sounded just right to her.

The counselor smiled and typed that in as well. "You are something special, you hear me."

"Thank you, and can you make my bio read: God is fighting your battles, arranging things in your favor, and making a way even when you don't see a way."

Counselor Eubanks looked up at Annabelle and said, "You going to probably be a preacher one day, you got that gift. Mark my words now."

Annabelle stood quiet, but she heard everything that counselor Eubanks said, then suddenly, a knock came from the other side of the door. She jumped nervously, and her eyes widened with fear. Counselor Eubanks tapped her and pointed at the trashcan. "Get the trash," she whispered.

Annabelle leaned down and pulled the trash bag out of the can, it was half full. Then the counselor said, "Come in." Her eyes were dead on the door.

The door came open, then walked in a tall caramel complexion man in a gray two-piece suit, hard bottom dress shoes and a fancy tie. He was one of the unit managers over the prison. He had rank, but not as much as the wardens.

"Good morning, ladies," his baritone voice bellowed. His eyes were on Counselor Eubanks. He stopped in front of her desk and Annabelle, on cue said, "Let me go take this trash out and put this mop bucket up." She walked out without saying another word and closed the door behind her, she pushed the mop and bucket down the hall to the closet, her heart was still racing because she knew she wasn't supposed to have been in there that long in the first place. Inside the closet, she poured out the dirty water and rinsed out the mop and hung it up.

She needed something to do, so she left the closet and walked down the hallway and sipped some water from the water fountain. She moved up front towards the windows and opened the blinds and looked out for a second. Just outside, she noticed several women prisoners walking by, some of them were heading to GED class, walking in line and dressed in their two-piece beige colored uniforms. Annabelle thought to herself, *I'm not supposed to be here. I'm not supposed to be here.* She repeated to herself. *God please remove me from this prison.* In her mind, she visualized that she was in a huge mansion, standing in her window looking out across the lake, she saw children playing, music was playing in the background.

She had on a white dress and was barefoot. There was thick white carpet underneath her feet. A white baby grand piano was to the right of her. Then she heard laughing. She snapped back from her daydream and turned around and saw the unit manager walking out of Counselor Eubanks' office. Then she noticed her head peep out of the door, she motioned her hand for Annabelle to come back. Annabelle walked towards her and on into the office. She closed the door behind her. Counselor Eubanks was back at her desk and on the computer.

"What I'm about to do now is send out some friend request for you."

"So, he didn't suspect anything?" she asked, referring to the unit manager.

"Of course not, why would he?" She smiled. "You ain't got to never worry about him. I got him wrapped around my finger, if you know what I mean."

"Well, I did see how he was looking at you, I'll assume that's your boyfriend."

"Close, more like my ex-husband, you haven't noticed that we have the same last name?"

Annabelle slapped her forehead when she thought about it and a smile appeared across her face. She looked at the computer screen. "Can I write something really quick?"

Counselor Eubanks stood up and said, "Sit down."

Annabelle's fear disappeared when she sat down and rolled the chair up closer the computer and began typing.

I was standing in my mama's kitchen, and it was hot for two reasons. One we didn't have an air condition and two the oven was on four hundred and fifty degrees with a ham baking inside. The aroma was wonderful, it had my stomach growling and my mouth watering. My mother was standing over the stove frying fatback and chopped onions, and the collard greens were simmering. She wiped her hands on her apron and said to me, "Daughter, I love." She never turned around, her back was to me, as she added the fatback and onions into the pot of collard greens. That made me smile and I walked over to her and wrapped my arms around her waist, laid my head against her back and I whispered, "I love you, too, Mama."

"Have you made the sweet tea yet?" she asked.

I pressed my head against my mother's back even harder, it was a moment that I had to enjoy, then I pulled away from her and said. "No ma'am, but I'm about to do it now." I went to the counter and pulled down the Dixie Crystal sugar bag and the box of Lipton tea, then there was a knock at the front door. "I'll get it, mama," I said to my mother and walked from the kitchen and through the hallway. Our floors were made of wood, and with every step I took, the floors creaked. When I got to living room, I saw a man standing on the front porch. The wooden door was opened and the only thing that separated him and me was the ragged screen door. When I got to the front door I noticed that I hadn't never seen the man before around the neighborhood. I stared at him from head to toe. He had a big tall afro and a beard that was thick. His shirt was dirty, the top three buttons were opened, he wore a dingy pair of corduroy pants in the summer. When I looked down at his feet, I noticed that he was barefooted. At the age of twelve, I didn't know what to say or think. My eyes went up to his and I said, "How you are doing, sir?"

"Well, I'm doing; I'm here. It took me a minute, but I've finally came."

I was confused as to what he was saying. And I guess it showed on my face. He then said to me. "May I have something to drink?"

Before I could answer, I heard my mama yell, "Who is it, daughter?"

I turned around as my momma approached. "It's a man, mama; he only wants something to drank," I said to her.

My mama stared down at me. I noticed that her eyes had narrowed, and from years of knowing my mama, that was a sign of her about to get mad.

"Fix him a glass of water, daughter," she said and walked up the hallway further into the living room. She eyed the man standing there in front of the screen door. Their eyes met for a few seconds and it seemed as if momma had seen a ghost, but she pushed the screen door open anyway. "Come on in," she said to him.

The man walked in, stood there near the threshold for a moment

and looked around at our front room. The furniture was covered with
thick plastic, and on the wooden coffee table were some pictures of
momma and I in frames. To the left was an open window with a box
shaped fan sitting inside of it spinning and cooling off the front room
only. He then looked at her and put out a huge dirty hand in her face.
"Thank you for welcoming me into your home."

"You're welcome."

I hurried off to get the stranger a drink. I was coming around the
corner with the ice-cold glass of water and a paper towel. My mama
always told me that I should use a paper towel when I fixed something
to drank just in case the glass started to sweat. When I finally got into
living room, I saw my mama and the man shaking hands. She must
have already known him from somewhere. Then I heard him say, "I'm
God, I was just in the neighborhood checking on my children and I
must say, this is the seventh house that I stopped by today. And you are
the first person to let me in." He then looked at me and said, "I didn't
make a mistake when I created you, I'm not going to stand here and tell
you that life is going to be a piece of cake for you. But I will most defiantly see you through it."

I stood there for a minute, then I walked up to him with glass of ice
water, with both hands I handed it to him. He let go of my mama hand
and he took the glass from me and said. "Thank you, my child."

"You're welcome, Father." I said to him, then I moved over to my
mama and put my arm around her waist. We stood there together and
watched him drank down the water. When he finished, he handed me
the glass and the only sounds that was heard was the ice cubes that
was rattling in the bottom of it. "I'm leaving now, but I'll be back soon,"
he said and then he was gone.

TO BE CONTINUED

Annabelle looked up at Counselor Eubanks and asked,
"What you think?" Her eyes went back to the computer screen for
a second and then back up to her. She saw counselor Eubanks

eyes getting moist. "I think it's wonderful and I also think that you are going to be very important one day. But before you post this, comment at the bottom to tell everyone to like your post, comments are welcome and please share."

Annabelle did what she was told, and after that, she posted it. "Well, here goes nothing." She smiled and clicked 'post.'

19

A week had passed, and Annabelle's Facebook page was up to almost four thousand followers, she had already hit her limit of five thousand friends and people from all over the world was engaging with her stories and inspirational quotes. When she finally got a chance to get to the computer, Counselor Eubanks said to her, "I just can't believe that all these people are following your story like this." She then pointed to the bottom of one of the post. "Fifteen hundred people shared this, eight hundred and seventy-three comments and twenty-two hundred likes." She stood up quickly. "Get to work, you got a hungry fan base."

Annabelle sat down, she thought about what she was about to write and started moving her fingers.

Two years went by quickly, I was now fourteen. Everyone was saying I was a big girl now, even though I didn't feel as if I had grown. On this particular day, I was sitting on the front porch with my mama watching the cars pass by. Our front porch was lined with flowers of all different types and my mama was in her rocking chair a few feet away from me. When I looked over at her, she was circling words in her seek and find magazine.

"Do you think God gonna come by today?" I asked her.

She was looking down in the magazine, her pen was in her hand. Then her head slowly rose up and she looked me in my eyes. "Even if He doesn't show up physically, He's here spiritually, look how peaceful it is," she said and looked around. She took a deep breath and closed her eyes, pretending to sniff the air. Then a square body Taxi cab pulled up in front of our house. It was a fat faced man behind the wheel, he had his hand hanging out of the window with a smoking cigar between his fingers. He looked at me. "Excuse me young lady, but I got message for you," he said to me.

I stood up and looked at my mama. The look she gave me said that it was alright to walk down the steps and to the car, so I proceeded, dressed in my old cut off blue jean shorts and a Tommy Hilfiger T-shirt and flip flops. I got down to the bottom step of my mama's front porch and then walked down the four concrete squares that led to the curb where the Taxi cab was parked. The driver switched his cigar to his other hand and then he handed me a white envelope. I looked at it on both sides and there was nothing written on it. The cab pulled off, and I turned around and headed back to the porch, and not paying attention to my steps, I tripped just as I got to the top step and bumped my knee. My face scrunched up at the little pain the impact had on my knee from the wooden porch.

"Careful baby. Pay attention to where you are going, daughter," my mama said.

"Yes ma'am," I said quickly getting up and went over and sat in the chair where I was sitting before going to the parked cab. I tore open the envelope, it was a letter inside, so I thought, but it was just a blank piece of paper with nothing written on it. I flipped it from front to back. Nothing.

I didn't get it, the cab driver said that he had a message for me, but it most certainly wasn't on the paper. I looked at my mama. "It's blank, mama," I said to her. "He said he had a message for me. I don't get it."

My mama slowly closed her magazine, she then turned her head *towards me, her stare was calm and warm. She then said, "You already received the message, daughter."*

I looked back at the paper again, I was confused. Then I examined the envelope, still nothing. I looked back at her and she said to me, "When you slipped, what did I say?"

I thought about it for a second or two, then it hit me. "Pay attention to where you are going, daughter," I said.

My mama head started moving up and down in a slow motion. "He works in mysterious ways, daughter, remember that," she said to me.

Thanks everyone for reading with me. I hope you all enjoyed the story that I shared. Please share, comment below and let me know what you think. And may God continue to bless us as a whole family.

Annabelle then hit the post button and sat back. Her eyes were on the screen, she saw the likes going up by the minute and the shares was already at thirty-three before she looked over her shoulder at the counselor.

The first comment read: God loves you, Sunday school teacher.

The next comment read: He's watching over all of us. Stay blessed. Whoever you are.

Annabelle smiled and nodded her head in agreement with the commenters. Some of the comments she responded back to and some she just read and smiled. The numbers were going up and up. Comment after comment, shares were up to seventy-eight in the first four minutes. She finally looked up at Counselor Eubanks again, but she was no longer standing there. Annabelle didn't panic, instead she started to type again.

Dear Father, Thank you for all the gifts and blessings that you pour into us as a family. And even more that you pour into me to enlighten your children's hearts and minds. Today, we walk as sisters and brothers in Christ. Let your love be strong and powerful as we allow it to come into us, come into our homes. I want to send a prayer up this morning for the homeless, for our brothers and sisters that are in prison and the wrongfully convicted. Touch them this morning, Father. Touch our sisters and brothers across the world that has fell victim to drugs. Touch the ones that are fighting for their lives, battling with cancer, heart disease and all things that we know you are capable of removing, Father. Together, our faith weighs ten tons and we're coming in unity to your Holy Spirit, Father; not just me, but your people, Father and we need you. We seek you, Lord, for comfort, understanding and help. It's millions of people praying with me, and we are ALL YOUR CHILDREN, in Jesus name. Amen.

Annabelle posted that post and then she logged off of her Facebook page and stood up. She walked towards the door and opened it, and when she stepped out into the hallway she looked in both directions. Counselor Eubanks wasn't anywhere in site, and Annabelle turned on her heels and headed down the hallway and towards the row of cubicles. She headed towards the doors that led to the chaplain area. It didn't take her long to get back to her dorm, she was buzzed through the sally port doors. In the middle of the day, the dayroom was nearly empty, there was a few women working out and that was one of the things that most women did in prison, everyone was competing with one another for the best shaped body. Annabelle went to her cell, which she shared it with an older white lady, and her cellmate never complained or was hardly ever in the room. Her new cellmate worked in the kitchen all day and that gave Annabelle a lot of time to herself.

The first thing that she did was took off her Reebok sneakers and sat down on the foot of her bed. She removed her pants and state issued shirt and slipped into a pair of gray gym shorts and laid down on the bed for a few minutes, she closed her eyes, she could feel the sleep coming down on her. All she needed was a nap, thirty minutes at the most, or at least that's what she thought anyway. After twenty minutes had passed, she was in a deep dream, and in her dream, she was inside a huge mega church called Word of Faith with thousands and thousands of people

clapping and cheering and praising God. The music was amazing, and the atmosphere was euphoric.

Annabelle was on the front row, but over to the left as if it was
her own private section. And sitting next to her was her friend,
Black Girl. She had her Bible on her lap, her head was slightly
bowed, and she was moving her lips and speaking in tongues.
Even Annabelle didn't understand what she was saying, she just
continued to give God praise.

"Wake up," a voice said to her.

Annabelle opened her eyes, she was indeed tired. She turned
over and saw Black Girl sitting there on the stool of the desk, her
Bible was sitting on her lap and opened. Annabelle sat up,
rubbed her eyes. "What time is it?" she asked.

"Almost ten."

"At night?"

"Of course, at night, you been out for a minute. You missed a
big fight earlier," she said, "But that wasn't important." She
turned a few pages in her Bible and she found opened the Bible
to the scripture Annabelle imagined she was looking for.
"Matthew 11:28," she said and then she began reading. "Come to
me, all you who are weary and burdened, and I will give you
rest." She looked at Annabelle and said, "Now, this really spoke to
me." She paused for a second. Then she went on. "On some real
sh— I mean stuff. I'm not tryin' to die in here."

"So, what are you going to do about it?"

Black Girl looked down, she raised her right hand. "I'm going
to do my time, stay outta trouble and get my life on track." She
shook her head, then she said, "Honestly, I'm really tryin' to get
myself together. And I remember you tellin' me that I could do
whatever I wanted to through Christ."

Annabelle got up out of her bunk and went over and took
both of Black Girl's hands in hers and she smiled. "And you can,
it may not come how you want it or as fast as you want it, but I'm
telling you, once you accept Jesus in your life as your Lord and

Savior, you're going to feel better. Blessings are gonna come so fast and big that you won't believe."

Black Girl took a deep breath. "I just don't want my situation to be like Samson, I mess around and drop my flag and lose all my strength."

Annabelle let out a laugh and shook her head. "Let me tell you how God works. Before you woke me up, I was just dreaming that we were in this huge mega church sitting next to one another. You were praying, and I was so proud of you. And now look how he manifests things in our favor." She stood up and Annabelle bent down and slipped on her shoes. "I got to go make a phone call."

Black Girl stood up, she gave Annabelle a warm hug. "I'll rather walk with God than put in work for the Devil. I'm getting too old for this gang bangin' foolishness."

"God's gang," Annabelle said.

"A whole lot of God gang it is," Black Girl said. Her smile was wide across her face.

Annabelle left her cell and went to the front of the dorm where the wall phones were. She got on one of them and dialed Daisy Mae's number. She waited for the boring operator to finish the terms and conditions of the call and then she heard her voice.

"Hey baby, God is good ain't He?" Daisy Mae said from the other end, but her voice was low and weak.

"Yes, He is," she said. "You don't sound too good, what's wrong?"

There was a long silence on the other end, then finally Daisy Mae said, "I got a lump on my bosom, at least that's what the doctor told me."

It felt as if Annabelle's entire body froze up when she said that. Her throat got dry and her eyes got moist all at the same time. She felt the butterflies in her stomach and it seemed as if her chest was getting tight. Then Daisy Mae said, "It's nothing life threatening I can tell you that, we are not about to speak that into the atmosphere."

Annabelle closed her eyes as the tears pushed through. Then she said, "The Lord is faithful, He strengthened you and protect you from any and all evil. Dear Father, please remove any illness and sickness from Sister Daisy's body, heal her Father. I need her here, and I need her healthy. We need her healthy." Then there was a long pause, Annabelle couldn't help it, she broke down in tears and finally said, "Amen."

"Thank you, baby," Daisy Mae whispered from the other end. Then she said, "I love you."

And the phone clicked, and the operator said, "This call has been terminated."

Annabelle took a deep breath and wiped her eyes with the sleeve of her t-shirt. She sniffed and fought hard to get herself together. Deep breath after deep breath and now it was to the point where she felt like it was a ton of weights on her back. She slowly hung up the phone, then she turned around, and just as she was about to head towards her cell, a short chubby girl with braids named Tee Mama walked up to her with a smile on her face. "Hey sexy red, I know this time gettin' to you." She touched Annabelle's face and wiped the tear that was rolling down her cheek. "Why don't you come to my room for a few minutes and let me ease your pain." Tee Mama pushed her up against the closest wall and continued feeling her up and whispering in her ear. She then turned Annabelle's face towards hers and kissed her on the lips.

Without warning, Annabelle side stepped and cocked her arm back, made a tight fist, bit down on her bottom lip and swung her arm like her life dependent on it. When her fist connected with Tee Mama's face it smashed her on her nose and she heard the crunch underneath her fist, she yelled out in pain like a wounded animal and blood poured like a running faucet from her face. Tee Mama bent over at the waist and covered her face with both hands. Annabelle backed up, she had blood splattered across the front of her white tee shirt. Then the front door of the dorm was buzzed open and four officers rushed in screaming. "Lock down, everybody to your cells. NOW!"

Then one of the female officers walked up to Annabelle. "Turn around, cuff up," she blasted to her and pulled out a pair of handcuffs.

Annabelle slowly turned around and put her hands behind her back. She closed her eyes as she felt the cold handcuffs closing in around her wrist. Two of the other officers got on each side of Tee Mama and they escorted her out first. Annabelle was looking around the dorm, and she saw Black Girl. She looked curious and Annabelle knew she wanted to know what happened, but she just shook her head and shrugged her shoulders. She may have overreacted, but Tee Mama had approached her sideways at the wrong time.

She mouthed the words, "I don't know." As they removed her from the common area and escorted her to the hole.

fter twenty-six days in lockdown, Annabelle was finally released, and she was in luck to be sent back to the same dorm that she left from nearly a month ago. Annabelle had lost about ten pounds and her skin complexion was nearly two shades lighter, her hair was a mess and all she wanted was a shower. When she got inside the dorm, carrying a net bag full of dirty clothes on her shoulder, she was met at the sally-port doors by Black Girl and she greeted her with a hug and a smile.

"Glad to see you back, are you alright?" Black Girl asked.

She picked up Annabelle's mattress from the floor and put it up on her shoulder.

"I'm glad to be back, and yeah, I'm alright."

"What room did they put you in?"

"Two-sixteen, upstairs." She began walking towards the stairs, and Black Girl was behind her. When they arrived at the room upstairs, Annabelle pulled the door open, and to her surprise the entire room was empty. That meant she didn't have a cellmate. She put her bag down and Black Girl sat her mattress on the bottom bunk. Then she looked at Annabelle. "I did it."

"You did what?" she asked.

"I got saved."

"Are you serious?" Annabelle smiled, her heart was smiling and just that fast she felt the joy running through her veins.

"I'm serious, I wouldn't play with you or God like that," she said and then added, "And I'm no longer affiliated with the gang, they removed me." She sounded sad, and it did hurt. The pain was shown all over her face. "So, it's just you, me and God, now."

Annabelle took a deep breath and grabbed her hands. "That's all we need."

"God's gang," Black Girl responded.

The following morning, Annabelle was up and ready to go up front to her detail, but the officer in the booth wouldn't let her out of the dorm. Annabelle was confused, trying to plead her case, she tried to tell the officer that she worked with the chaplain and the counselors. The officer still refused to let her out. Annabelle was getting frustrated, so she took a deep breath to calm herself. She noticed that the officer lady was on the phone. She was looking at her through the thick glass window and she was laughing. That was a good sign. Then suddenly the door buzzed, and Annabelle walked out.

It only took her about five minutes to get up to the front hall. Annabelle was fresh that morning, her pants were ironed, she had her hair combed and pulled back into a tight ponytail and her face was clean and she wore a small touch of makeup. Walking with confidence, she knocked on the Counselor Eubanks' door.

"Come in." She heard her say from the inside.

Annabelle turned the doorknob and slowly pushed the door open, when she saw Counselor Eubanks they both smiled at the same time. She jumped up from her seat and nearly ran around the desk and gave Annabelle a quick hug. "I'm glad you're back, but I'm disappointed in you," she said.

"I figured you would be, but I had a lot on my mind when she stepped to me and one thing led to another."

"Well, at least you won; I heard about you," she said with a smile.

Annabelle smiled. "Yes, I did that."

Counselor Eubanks nodded and pulled Annabelle over towards the computer. "I got a surprise for you," she said. She logged in to Annabelle's Facebook page and when she looked down, Annabelle noticed that she had just a little over one million followers on her page. "Oh, my God," she said in pure shock and covered her mouth and nose with her hands.

"Is this for real?" she asked.

"One point one million people from all walks of life are waiting for you to say something. Tuh, I'm waiting for you to say something." She smiled at her.

Annabelle's heart was racing, and she couldn't believe it. She sat down in the swivel chair and thought about what she was about to type. She took a breath so deep that her chest puffed up like she was waiting to be enlisted into the Army.

First off, allow me to thank God for allowing my words to touch over one million people, correction, God's children. I'm not sure where I would be without you guys support. Secondly, if you are following The Sunday School teacher's page, I need my prayer warriors to send up a big prayer with me for a woman that's so dear to me. I love her like she's the woman that brought me into this world. We are asking God to remove any illnesses from her body. When you like my post, comment and share, I feel like we're all holding hands and joining in with prayer together. Also, I have some wonderful news, I just brought a new family member home with us; she was saved a few weeks ago and she says she's no longer a gang member unless God has a gang. I told her yes. Hopefully, I answered her right. Amen to that. One day, I'll be allowed to share my world with y'all so you can really know who I am and what I've been through and the day to day struggle that I'm still going through. So please don't think that I am perfect. I'm logging off for now, and hopefully, if I have time, I'll be able to respond to some of the inbox messages. *Big kisses and hugs to each and every last one of you.*

Annabelle sat back and reread what she had just written, and she posted it. She then looked up at Counselor Eubanks and smiled. "What you think?"

"I think you are God's number one Angel," she said. "This is amazing."

Annabelle went inside the message box and noticed that there was well over five thousand unread messages, she didn't know where to start. She began strolling through some without even opening them. Then one particular one caught her eye. She opened it up and began reading: *Hello, my name is Daniel and I'm from London. As of now, I'm in a drug rehab. It's pretty expensive but that isn't what got me ready to get myself together. I've been following your page since you first started, and I will and must say that your messages and stories about God has truly been an inspiration to me. And I would love to come see you if it's not a problem. Hopefully, I don't sound like a stalker, and if I do, I'm truly sorry about that. I just know that we must meet one another face-to-face. I pray that you respond back to me. Thanks.*

Annabelle smiled and just shook her head. Then she hit the block button on his name. "Thanks, but no thanks," she said. But in her mind, she was thinking that the message was from someone that was just trying to pick her. She knew with over one million people following her that someone was probably an officer that was at the prison where she was. It seemed as if it was beginning to be a little too much and paranoia started to kick in, and she looked at Counselor Eubanks. "I think we need to delete this page. I just got a feeling that whoever that was is trying to see what's going on," Annabelle said, and took a deep breath and waited for Counselor Eubanks to respond.

"Fine, if that's what you want." She moved over to the computer, she had had a disappointed look over her face.

Without another word, she deactivated The Sunday School Teacher's page and looked at Annabelle. "Done," was all she said.

"Thank you," Annabelle said and walked out of her office without saying another word.

§♠

AS THE WEEKS PASSED, ANNABELLE HAD REMOVED HERSELF FROM the detail up front and just focused on her legal work and did Bible study with Black Girl and a few more women around the prison. It was more of what she liked, the Facebook page was changing her, and Annabelle was comfortable with being private, even though throughout the prison she was still popular because she was spreading the word of God. Day in and day out it was her and Black Girl that brought out at least fifty women of all colors in their Bible study classes and everyone was enjoying it and every other day one of the ladies was giving their lives to Christ. That was a blessing within itself.

The next morning, Annabelle was sitting out in the day room with Black Girl, and another lady named Sally. Sally was white with a face full of freckles and long red hair. They were all having coffee and talking when Annabelle's name was called on the intercom.

"Annabelle Humphrey, report to the Warden's office."

Annabelle looked back at the officer's booth, with her face twisted up a little because most times, if someone's name was actually called to come to the warden's office, it was something terribly wrong. She looked at Black Girl.

"What you think they are calling me for?" she asked her.

Black Girl seemed just as clueless as Annabelle and shrugged her shoulders.

"You said you deleted the Facebook page, right?"

"Yes, and that's been almost three months now. So, I definitely don't think it's that," she said.

Then Sally said, "Well, let's say a quick prayer for something good." The three of them joined hands and Sally softly prayed, "Dear Father, walk with our sista, Annabelle, as she goes to receive her blessing and wonderful news, in the Lord Jesus/ name we pray, Amen."

"Amen," Annabelle and Black Girl said in unison.

Ten minutes later, Annabelle was up front, sitting in a chair in the hallway just outside of the warden's office, and she was nervous as all outdoors. When the door opened, a tall mean looking cert team officer dressed in all black walked out and looked at Annabelle.

"You Humphrey?" he asked in a deep southern drawl, looking down at her as if she was guilty of something.

"Yes sir, I am," she said. Her stomach was twisting in knots and doing backwards flips and somersaults all at once.

"Come on in, Warden Brown wanna see you."

Annabelle stood up and walked inside of the warden's office. Her eyes landed on a dark-skinned burly man sitting behind his nice mahogany desk. He was staring at his computer and didn't look at her one time and she had always heard that he had a nasty attitude.

"Have a seat," he said.

"Thank you, and good morning, Warden Brown," she said politely to try and ease the tension from the office.

"Morning," was all he said, then after a few brief moments he finally looked at her and said, "I've been hearing that you are pretty popular around my prison."

"I'm just a child of God, and all I do is spread the word."

"But from what I'm hearing, you have turned a lot of gang members into Christians and to follow your new so-called 'God Gang.'"

"That's not true, well not how you're putting it. We call ourselves sisters in Christ, because that's who we are."

"Well, where is all this money coming from for you to hire an entire team of high priced attorneys from Atlanta?" he asked in a low deep drawl.

Annabelle frowned with a confused look across her face.

"I don't have an attorney, I sent some letters in for the indigent defense team, some of them did respond back, but as far as money to hire them, I'm not sure what you are talking about."

The warden leaned back in his swivel chair with the tips of his fingers pressed together and he just stared at Annabelle as if she was lying.

"So, you didn't hire these lawyers?"

"What lawyers? I don't even know what you are talking about, sir."

"It's a team of lawyers here, in the special visiting area waiting to see you. And they big time because they contacted the Governor before they arrived, and they want to see Annabelle Humphrey."

Annabelle sat quiet for a moment, with her eyes locked on the warden. She was waiting for what he had to say next, because she clearly didn't know what was going on.

Then the warden said, "I'm going to let you see them. Escort her around there."

"Follow me, Humphrey," he said.

Annabelle stood up and turned towards the door, and soon as she was about to walk out the Warden said, "Humphrey."

Annabelle stopped and looked back at him. "Yes."

"Don't make my prison look bad, okay?" He pointed his finger.

She smiled. "Okay." Then she turned and followed the huge cert team officer down the hallway with a million things going on in her mind and the only thing she kept saying in her head was, Thank you, Jesus.

When the cert team officer got to the door of the room on the end, he twisted the knob and pushed the door open for her.

"I'll be standing right out here," he said to her.

"Okay." Anabelle walked inside the square room that was covered with carpet. There were four well-dressed white men sitting around a circular wooden table. Each of them wore smiles as they watched her walk in the door. Annabelle's eyes shifted from the first to the last one and back to the first one again. He rose to his feet, he was a muscular man, she could tell underneath his expensive dark gray suit. His hair was shiny and combed in a fashionable style.

"Good morning, Miss Humphrey, my name is Eugene Wolfe and I was hired to represent you until you are fully released from prison," he said. "Nice to meet you."

"Nice to meet you as well." She shook his hand. He sat down and the next gray-haired gentlemen that resembled Santa Clause stood up with an outstretched hand. Annabelle stepped in front of him.

"Hello, Miss Humphrey. It's a pleasure to meet you. I'm attorney Bryan Winston of Winston and Winston law firm in Atlanta."

Annabelle's butterflies were slowly disappearing, and she was starting to feel comfortable. The next handsome guy with gray eyes, a neatly trimmed full beard and a long ponytail introduced himself. When he gave Annabelle his hand, she noted that his grip was strong, and she admired how his tailored made suit fit him to perfection.

"I'm Bryan Winston Junior. My father and I normally don't work on the same cases together but the person that hired us to represent you, wanted the best, so you get the both of us." He smiled beautifully. *He was definitely attractive for a white man,* Annabelle thought.

"But I'm lost. I don't even know who hired you all to represent me. Do you all know?" she quizzed. Everybody got quiet for some reason, then they all looked to their left at the last guy that was still sitting down, he was examining Annabelle from head to toe. She moved down in front of him and he stood up, it was something different about him from the other three attorneys. He was about six feet even, had an even tan that had his skin a golden bronze. He was physically fit, with the build of a college defensive safety. He wore glasses, and he was clean shaven, with no facial hair. His hair was curly and auburn, and he was dressed in a two-piece suit, no tie. A regular tee shirt underneath and a pair of tennis shoes.

"Good morning, Annabelle," he said with a thick French accent and then he gave her his hand and she shook it.

"Good morning," she replied. Her heart was racing at a faster pace than it was when she first walked in the room. However, she did notice that he was the only one that addressed her by her first name.

"I'm Daniel," he said, and he stood there with an easy smile.

"Okay, how you doing, Daniel?" she asked him while staring in his eyes.

Daniel looked at the three attorneys. "Gentlemen, if you would. Give me a little time."

The three of them got up out their chairs without exchanging one word and they all exited the room. Daniel walked over to the door and closed it, and when he came back around, he sat on the edge of the table in front of Annabelle and folded his arms across his chest.

"So, I finally get to meet the Sunday school teacher," he said with a smile across his face.

Annabelle's heart nearly fell to the pit of her stomach, and she was so nervous that her hands began to shake. She was numb, and her words were trapped in her throat and all she could do was stare at him.

"I was one of your followers on Facebook," he whispered.

Annabelle swallowed. "Okay," she said.

"I sent you a message, I told you that I was in a rehab in London and that I wanted to come and see you." He smiled. "But then you blocked me, and I was so hurt after that."

Annabelle's hands went up to her face, she covered her mouth and a muffled whisper came. "Oh, my God." Her eyes were nearly in tears. "Are you serious? I'm so sorry, I was just..."

"Paranoid," he laughed, and then he added, "Yes, having so many followers when you were not supposed to have a page, would make one a bit paranoid."

"But...how did you find me?" she asked.

"Well actually, I got an inbox message from your page, but it was from Counselor Eubanks. She told me everything and the reason why you blocked me and shut down the page. Then she told me about you and your situation. I asked her to send me her phone number because I really wanted to meet the Sunday school teacher. After we talked over the phone, I told her the impact that you had on my life and that I wanted to help you. So here I am, I flew in from London to Atlanta yesterday, and I brought the best legal team to help with your appeal."

Annabelle was listening, but she thought her ears were playing tricks on her. The words his soothing voice spoke brought tears to her eyes and she didn't bother to wipe her wet cheeks. She felt her knees getting weak and she fell forward into Daniel's arms. He hugged her and held on to her.

"I don't even know what to say besides thank you," she cried.

"Well, you can also say that you will let me walk this path with you. I want you to put me on your visitation list. I'll come see you every two weeks until I get you home. God sent me to you, please don't deny me," he said while still holding her in his strong arms.

Annabelle exhaled and then stepped back from Daniel's embrace and looked up at him. The scent that he wore was lingered in the air and it smelled glorious. "I will not deny you, Daniel," she said, and just then, the emergency alarm went off. And when that alarm sounded it meant one or two things. Either an inmate had escaped, or it was a riot about to kick off.

Annabelle looked at the door when it opened. Not surprised, it was the big cert team guy.

"We got an emergency, she gonna have to go back to her dorm," he said to Daniel.

Daniel looked at Annabelle's kind eyes and then he grabbed her hand.

"I'll see you soon. I got you the best lawyers in the state of Georgia and I'm going to get you out of here," he said and added, "And that's a promise." His French accent sounded so good when he said that.

"Miss Eubanks has my number, talk to her," he said and then Annabelle was hauled off to her cell.

Annabelle was on cloud nine all the way to the dorm, and she couldn't wait to get back to the dorm to share the news with Black Girl and the rest of her sisters. When she made it back to her dorm, all ranks, including the warden was in her dormitory. Annabelle was escorted to her cell by the cert officer. Once they closed her door, she knew they'd be on lockdown. She looked at her roommate who was sitting on her bed.

"What happened around here?" she asked.

"They did that poor girl so bad, they didn't have to do her like that," she whimpered.

Annabelle's eyebrows bunched together.

"What happened?" she asked again, hoping her cellmate would give her more details.

"Your friend, Black Girl," she sniffled. "The Bloods came in the dorm, caught her while she was in her cell praying, they stabbed her up over twenty times, and the officers said that she's not going to make it."

Annabelle couldn't believe her ears, and she just knew she had to be mistaken. *No way was that accurate information,* was the thoughts that kept going through her head. But then she remembered the yellow tape that was down on the bottom range at Black Girl's door. Annabelle went to the door, she looked out through the small square window. Then she began beating with all her might.

"Hey, please. Help her!" she continued to yell and bang, but the officers didn't pay her any attention. There was so much noise from the other women banging, screaming and yelling also that it was just impossible for them to hear her pleas. Annabelle screamed and kicked until she didn't have any more energy in her. She took deep breaths to calm herself. She didn't know how long she had been banging to no avail, before she turned her back against the door and slid down to the floor in tears. She closed her tiny hands into fist and squeezed them as hard as she possibly could. She looked up towards the ceiling of the cell and opened her eyes as the tears streamed down her face. "Why God...Whhhyyyy?" she yelled to the top of her lungs. "Everything was going so good, how could you let this happen?" She then dropped her head and stared down at the floor and allowed the tears to pour from her face.

Then she heard a voice rumble.

"I didn't say that weapons wouldn't form, Annabelle. I only said that they wouldn't prosper."

TO BE CONTINUED...

AUTHOR'S NOTE

I know this story is far from the type of books that I've written in the past or what you are use to reading from me. And to my urban fiction, street literature and urban romance fans and supporters, I sincerely apologize to anyone that purchased it just because it had Cole Hart's name on it, and honestly, I was left with no choice but to write it. See, I learned the craft of writing books and storytelling while I was incarcerated and serving a life sentence. Several people had asked me what got me into writing while I was incarcerated and the only response that I could tell them is that it's truly a blessing from God. I've written at least twenty novels while I was in prison and this particular story about Annabelle Humphrey has been on my mind and heart since 2012, when I really started to read the Bible and getting myself, my life, my heart right with God. I created this young lady and her struggles in this story because I know somewhere in the world, it's sisters and brothers that's going through a struggle in life. Me personally, I went through one, nineteen years straight and hearing the phrases like: Brah, you ain't never going home: And if you do, you'll have to do at least twenty-five years. Well, neither one of those statements were true and I've been home six months. I made it my business to write this story because I prayed over it and gave myself my word, I gave my brothers that I left behind my word, and most importantly, I gave God my word that I would write this story once I was released. Now, this is the first book that I have ever written without a cuss word. That took something. I do consider this book urban and also Christian fiction. I'm currently writing part 2 right now, and I'm sure somebody wants to see what's going on with Annabelle, Black Girl and this good dude, Daniel, that just came all the way from London. Me personally, I'm waiting myself. Lol. Allow me to say thank you to everyone and I really appreciate your support. I'll always send a prayer up for the brothers and sisters that's incarcerated. Someone was praying for me and I know prayer works.

Also, if I'm not asking too much, please do me a favor and leave me a review on Amazon.com and let me know your thoughts on The Sunday School Teacher. It's a lot of truth to this story, even though its fiction. And the REAL PART is that God freed me from prison and gave me a second chance to be back with my family. I can never thank Him enough for that.

Thank you for taking the time to read with me and listen to me for a moment, and thanks again for leaving your review. Thank you again for your support. And most importantly, God Bless you.

CPSIA information can be obtained
at www.ICGtesting.com
Printed in the USA
LVHW032019200519
618482LV00002B/297/P

9 781726 633772